Slightly Spooky Stories III

Patsy Collins

Contents

1. Hunting The Haunters

Bradley wasn't the only one to gasp when Laura yanked the velvet drape off the stereo system. She pressed 'play' to reveal how the eerie voices from 'beyond the grave' had been channelled into the world of the living.

"Madame Giselle must have a remote control hidden in that cape," Laura explained.

For a moment Bradley was disappointed. Ever since he'd heard the story of the girl who could turn to mist and disappear, he'd been hoping to get a scoop on a real ghost, or failing that someone who could at least contact those who were no longer living. Madame Giselle, it had just been convincingly revealed, was not such a person.

The séance turned into something closer to a riot as people angrily demanded their money back and threatened to sue Madame Giselle. Bradley, realising this was still a good story for the family run local paper, gave out business cards saying he'd like to interview those who'd attended the meeting.

"I'll talk to you. She's been conning my mum out of money for months," one lady said.

"Me too. She lied to me about Arthur, that was just cruel."

Bradley scribbled down notes as fast as he could until he saw Laura quietly slip away from the room.

"Please give me a call and I'll ring you straight back, or

call into the office if you prefer," he told the crowd before following her. "Excuse me," Bradley called. "Laura, please wait."

At first he thought she was going to ignore him, but after a few more strides she slowed and allowed him to catch up.

"That was brilliant," he said. "The way you exposed her."

"I couldn't let her continue. She told so many lies about the dead and not just because she was trying to offer comfort as some people do, but to make a profit even if it hurt people."

"She's a nasty piece of work even by con artist standards. I think she'll get her comeuppance this time though. Arthur's brother was there, as well as his widow, and he's a lawyer."

"Yes, I know."

"There's a lot you know, isn't there?"

Laura had quite a reputation for exposing fake mediums, haunted houses which were simply draughty and those who claimed to be spiritualists, but were nothing of the sort. If she claimed an ability or phenomenon to be fake that was always proved to be the case. If she couldn't disprove the claims made by those in touch with the other side, then neither did anyone else.

"I'd like to work with you, exposing the frauds. I'm sure The News could help by contacting witnesses and things and we can pay you for every case we cover."

"I'm not interested in money, only in the truth."

"OK then. Will you help me print the truth?"

"Print the truth, or print whatever will sell papers?"

"The truth. My grandfather started this paper with the aim of spreading information, not lies. Sure he wanted to make a living and so do I, but an honest one. I'll promise you what I promised him; if I don't believe it's true I won't print it."

She looked thoughtful for a minute, then nodded.

Bradley told her that he'd been invited to a preview of the ghost walks at Solent Castle.

"I've been there. I think you'll be disappointed," Laura said.

"The new owners have spent a lot of money on it recently. They say it's haunted by Roundheads and are obviously hoping I'll do a piece on it, saying that's the case."

"Ah, then it's them who are going to be disappointed."

"You don't think there are any ghosts there?"

"Not any more, but let's find out shall we?"

As they approached the castle a few days later Bradley shivered. "Certainly looks creepier after dark."

"It's just how they've lit it."

He looked again at the dramatic shadows and the way crumbling turrets and hideous gargoyles were picked out. "You're right."

Bradley and Laura were welcomed and shown into a bright hall warmed by a huge log fire. They were given a glass of sweet mulled wine and a grisly talk on the history of the castle.

"Mostly true, I think," he told Laura. "Exaggerated for effect and we're yet to find out if those soldiers are really still here." He finished his drink. "Nice touch that, the mulled wine."

"You can have mine if you like. I'm not a fan of the stuff. I suppose they feel they have to give something to justify the ticket price."

"They haven't convinced you there are ghosts here yet, then?"

"The only thing that will convince me is actually meeting a ghost."

The tours started soon enough, with visitors being sent off in small groups, 'So as not to overwhelm the spirits.'

Laura made a peculiar choking sound.

"What's wrong?" As Bradley turned to her he saw Laura was trying to suppress a laugh.

"Come on, do you really think long dead Roundhead soldiers, who've done all the stuff we've just been hearing about, are going to be frightened of a few tourists? It's just because people feel less scared in larger groups."

Their guide introduced himself as Peter and asked, "Do you want all the grim, gory details, or shall I spare you the worst of it?"

"Tell us everything," a large lady, dressed in in a blood red coat, demanded.

"Everyone happy with that?" Peter asked.

Bradley, Laura and the rest of their group said they were.

"Excellent!" Peter led them out of the hall into a cold, dark passageway.

The contrast with the warm, bright hall was very effective and clearly done deliberately.

"We're now going to climb the East Tower. During the last battle here, these walls would have run with the blood of those who'd tried to find refuge in the tower."

They were taken up a gloomy spiral staircase. The lady in red was ahead of Bradley. She shuddered when she put her hand on the slimy, wet walls for support. Laura's cynicism must have been rubbing off on him because Bradley thought that should have been dealt with during the restoration project, or possibly it had, as he didn't remember any damp walls when he'd visited as a child.

"This tower was the last part of the castle to be captured," Peter told them. "The soldiers who tried to take refuge here were hacked to pieces, or thrown to their deaths." He directed his powerful torch onto the courtyard far below them. Then he turned off the inside lights so they could get a good view down over the rest of the eerily illuminated castle. As he continued to talk about the battle, his audience had no trouble seeing the physical damage which had resulted. It wasn't difficult to imagine such violence might have left other reminders, possibly in the spirits of those who'd committed those awful acts.

As they climbed back down the stairs, the sticky walls glistened. When they reached the bottom Bradley looked around at the pale faces of his companions.

"Everyone all right?" Peter asked.

They all said they were, although some sounded just a little unsure.

"I want you to remember that these soldiers don't see you as the enemy. You may feel their cold touch as they try again and again to flee the castle, but they won't hurt you."

The small group were taken down a passageway.

"Just to our left is the entrance to the dungeon. Work is still ongoing to restore that area. It's taking time because we've discovered several skeletons. The bones had been gnawed by rats." Peter smiled, showing his teeth. "We assume it happened after death, or perhaps hope is more accurate."

Bradley shuddered. "He's very good," he whispered to Laura.

"He's certainly plenty scary enough."

Every now and then someone gasped because they thought they'd seen something in an alcove or walkway leading off from their route. On one occasion the lady who wanted to hear every horrible detail screamed, making Laura drop her bag.

"It's OK, he won't hurt you," the guide reminded them all, as he beckoned them to follow him around the next corner.

By the time they assembled in the next area, an armoury, Bradley saw Laura had her bag again. He felt guilty. He should have gone back to fetch it for her; obviously she'd felt nervous or she wouldn't have dropped it.

Peter paced about the room, pointing out displays of horrific weapons as he continued his gruesome talk. When he mentioned a sword he mimed the action of swinging it at head height to decapitate an enemy. He twisted his hands as he described the use of the disembowelling spike. The castle didn't need a ghost, Bradley thought; Peter was doing a terrific job of bringing the horrible past to life.

At one point Bradley suddenly felt icy cold just for a moment. It was an unnerving experience.

"Did you feel that? The red coated lady asked. "I felt one of them run right through me!"

"Oh, Bradley this is too much for my nerves," Laura wailed. "Take me back to the car, please."

Despite his concern for her, Bradley couldn't help being excited that the castle really did seem to be haunted. "Of course."

"I'll radio for someone to come and take you back," Peter

said. "Would you like to sit down while we wait?" He seemed really concerned and tactfully didn't remind Laura that he'd given them all the opportunity to avoid hearing the more bloodthirsty elements of his talk.

"No, thank you. I don't want to make a fuss," Laura said. "If you can just point us in the right direction." She produced a torch from her bag and gave a brave smile.

As soon as they were headed back to the car and out of sight of the guard Laura stopped trembling.

"Feeling better?" Bradley asked. He was wondering if it would be heartless to leave her in the car with the lights, heater and radio all on, while he rejoined the group.

"I'm fine. Can you see a way back in?"

Oh good, it seemed she wouldn't mind him returning. "I'll find one, but let's get you back to the car first."

"I'm coming with you. If you fell for my act back there you're obviously not good at spotting a fake."

"Oh. No ghosts?"

"Not a one. Get us back into the passageway where I dropped my bag and I'll show you."

Once they reached the spot where the lady had screamed, Bradley saw what had alarmed her. A ghostly apparition seemed to leap out at him. Laura held her torch for him to investigate. Soon he spotted an electric fan recessed into the wall and above him, on a wire, hung a model of a soldier crafted from tissue paper and thin strips of nylon.

"With the fan on this would move forward and flutter. If you just catch a glimpse as you pass by it works really well," he said.

"I think there are a few. My guess is they're on timers so just one or two people see something but it seems to have gone if anyone tries to take a closer look."

They continued on to the armoury.

"Stand where you were when you felt cold and tell me what you remember," Laura instructed.

"I was here, I think and the guide was showing us the …" He reminded himself she hadn't really been frightened. "He showed us the disembowelling spike."

Laura stepped toward the spike. As she did, Bradley heard a hiss and experienced that unpleasant icy blast again.

"There's a button on the floor here," she explained. "When I tap it with my foot it releases compressed, chilled air." She did it again.

"With him talking we didn't hear the hiss."

"Exactly. So are you going to expose them?"

He'd have to of course; they were intending to deceive the public who'd be expected to pay a high price for the privilege. He wouldn't be party to that. It was a shame though as the company concerned had done an excellent job of the restoration. It must have cost a huge sum so he didn't begrudge them trying to recover that if they were to do it honestly. The castle was providing much needed jobs for local people, and a successful tourist attraction would be good for the whole town's economy. And the tour had been entertaining in a horrible kind of way.

"What if we got them to admit the truth?" he asked.

"That they're cheating people?"

"They haven't yet, have they? Not really. There's a question and answer session at the end. The manager could tell everyone before they left."

"If they can continue to look after the castle and provide jobs without making false claims about the spirit world then that's OK with me."

He grinned. If Laura could see so clearly what was on his mind then surely he could convince the manager.

They returned to the hall in which they'd been welcomed and found staff setting out snacks and more glasses.

"I need to see your boss," Bradley said.

The manager arrived, shook his hand warmly and asked, "If you'd like pictures for the paper I can provide you with plenty and if there's anything else you need to ask …"

The man looked from Bradley to Laura and back again. The smile fell from his face.

It only took Bradley a few minutes to persuade him to come clean. Well, sort of. Once everyone returned from their tours he told them that a few special affects had been employed to add to the experience. He asked them to return the promotional literature. "The current versions are a little misleading. We'll have them reprinted and sent out to you before the official opening."

Bradley worked with the owners to help word posters and adverts in such a way that encouraged visitors who wanted ghostly thrills, without making false claims.

"Is that good enough?" he asked Laura. "At least one person left convinced she'd really felt a ghostly presence."

"That people aren't lied to is enough, I think. You can't control what people actually believe, as often it's just whatever they want the truth to be. And who knows, maybe amongst the fake roundheads there was a real ghost from a different time?"

Bradley shrugged. He still wanted to believe ghosts were real, but was beginning to think he'd never find proof.

"Do you have another project in mind?" Laura asked.

He did but was now reluctant to say. So many people had written to the paper praising the abilities of Serena South, saying how much she'd helped them with their grief, he thought there was a chance she really possessed a gift and could contact those who'd crossed over. He'd so wanted Laura to prove Serena genuine, he'd convinced himself that would happen. But that was before they'd gone to Solent Castle. Now he thought he'd rather be unsure than know Serena was another fake.

"I can see you do," Laura prompted.

"OK, yes I do. But this person doesn't charge anything, so she's not cheating anyone."

"Some of these people claim not to charge, but then the dearly departed suggest the bereaved person give a little gift, or sometimes they resort to blackmail."

"I'm fairly sure Serena South doesn't do that."

"Oh Serena! Yes, I agree."

"You don't think we'd be able to expose her as a fake?"

"Absolutely not. If she's genuine there's nothing to expose."

"You think she really talks to dead people?"

"Yes, of course she does." Laura sounded so sure.

Maybe she was just telling him what he wanted to hear. She did have an uncanny ability to guess what he was thinking. "Have you talked to her?"

"No, but I know people who have."

"You know people who said they'd seen a ghost at Solent Castle too."

"Said they had, yes."

"So you discover the truth by working out if people are

lying?"

"I suppose that helps, but sometimes people really believe they've seen, or spoken to, dead people. That lady at the castle for example. If she tells people a ghostly soldier walked right through her she'd be wrong, but would she be lying?"

"No, not exactly."

Bradley was confused. Did that mean Laura felt Serena South was an accidental fraud? No, hadn't she said the woman really did talk with the dead? It was no good, he'd have to investigate the spiritualist.

"Will you come with me to see Serena?"

"If you like, but you won't get to expose her as a fraud because she isn't."

"No problem. I'll reveal her to be genuine and you can help me prove it."

"You'll find that's not so easy."

Serena happily agreed to meet him and said she hoped she'd be able to answer his questions. When he arrived with Laura though, the lady seemed perturbed. Bradley guessed she'd recognised Laura and was anxious she'd be exposed. Was he never going to find any genuine ghosts or people in contact with them?

"Serena is more likely to be able to help if you tell her the truth, Bradley," Laura said.

Bradley explained why he was there, including the admission he'd expose her in the paper if he believed her to be a fraud.

"I'm happy to talk to you, but it might be better if Laura leaves. Her presence might make it harder for me to hear the voices which will convince you I'm genuine."

Had Bradley used Laura's name? He didn't think so, but Serena might have known it already. She might have known about his grandfather starting the paper and training young Bradley too. It was possible she could, if she'd put in a lot of effort, have learned many of the things she told him. Not all though. He hadn't told anyone what happened the night his father told him he couldn't keep running the paper. Bradley's mum was sick and he wanted to spend his time with her, not at work.

Bradley had gone to the newspaper offices that night and sat on his grandfather's old chair. He'd sat there as a kid, playing with a box of letters that had formed part of the press when Grandfather first published the paper. The box was still there somewhere Bradley knew. He found it at last on a high shelf. As he brought it down, letters spilled out. They'd landed on the cracked lino floor spelling out, 'Your turn now Bradley'.

Remembering Grandfather's insistence on correct English at all times, Bradley couldn't resist finding a comma and placing it before his name so the phrase was grammatically correct. Then he'd put the letters away where he'd found them and gone home to tell his father he'd take over the paper.

Serena continued talking. She assured him that his mother's recovery was complete and she had many happy years ahead of her. She said how proud his grandfather was of him and mentioned further details known only to himself. Bradley had no doubt that Serena really was in contact with his grandfather.

Laura clearly wasn't at all surprised to hear that. Neither did she seem surprised at the reaction his newspaper report on Serena received. Some people wrote in saying that although Bradley himself might believe what he'd written, they weren't so gullible. Clearly he'd been brainwashed or tricked in some way. Others did believe him, but they were the same people who'd always considered Serena to be genuine.

"You were right," he told Laura. "I know she's genuine, but I can't prove it and I've not convinced a single person."

"Never mind, you told the truth and sold lots of copies of the paper. That's your job, right?"

"Yes, I suppose so."

"You're a good man, Bradley and good at your job."

"Thanks. You're good at what you do too. Can you tell me how you do it?"

"It's easy when you know who to ask."

"Go on."

She looked thoughtful.

"Off the record if you like. I want to know, even if I can't print what you tell me."

"I'm not worried about you printing anything about me, just trying to think of a way to explain. OK, suppose someone says, as Serena did, that they've talked to your grandfather. The only way I can be sure that's true is to ask him. By the way, he said to tell you to go easy on the exclamation marks."

"You can talk to him too?"

She smiled by way of an answer.

"And the ghosts?"

"I just ask them. A blast of compressed air, or paper model blown by an electric fan can't tell me their story. Real spirits can. Sometimes I find out why they're haunting the place and help them leave if that's what they want. Sometimes they choose to stay."

He wanted her to be right, but hadn't she told him herself that people sometimes believed what they wanted to? "How come you're so sure you're right? You could be conned, or fooling yourself."

She gave that smile again. Then she slowly grew paler and less substantial until all Bradley could see was a misty outline of the girl. Then even the mist was gone.

Bradley had seen his ghost. He didn't print the story though; no one would believe him.

2. Come And Find Me

I let myself into my parent's house and called out a greeting.

"Kettle's just boiled," Mum replied.

I took my mug of tea into the lounge. They weren't there.

"Through here, Julie love," Mum said.

No big deal, they were in the dining room. Even so that small thing unsettled me. Or perhaps I was just a bit on edge because I hadn't been sleeping well?

Mum and Dad were studying a mass of paperwork, including bank statements.

"Something wrong?" I asked. As far as I knew they had plenty of money. They've always been generous to their only child. When I accepted the down payment for my flat I'd guessed perhaps I was spending part of my inheritance, but it never occurred to me I might be leaving them short of cash.

"Some lowlife has cloned one of our bank cards and been helping himself," Dad said. "The bank spotted it quickly, but we've got to check they didn't miss anything. While we're at it, we thought we'd make sure everything else is in order."

"Can I help?"

Everything seemed fine, but one regular payment puzzled me. It was a standing order to a self storage company. The house isn't as large as the one we moved out of after… When I was seven, but it's still got plenty of space.

My finger rested by the entry on their bank statement, but

my mouth wouldn't ask the question. I could feel them hesitate. Knew they looked for signs that the other would tell me.

Mum gulped in air and let it out with a whisper. "It's for your sister's things."

How could they keep memories of her? I'd made myself forget. It was better that way.

They explained my distress had been so great whenever I saw anything of hers, or anyone mentioned her, they'd decided to move away from the memories.

"You wouldn't go to the park where you both used to play or enter schoolrooms where she'd been taught. When you passed her room you kept so far from the door and rushed by so fast, we worried you'd take a tumble down the stairs."

I wasn't really listening. The memories wouldn't stay hidden. My big sister Lucinda. I'd wanted to be with her constantly, share the things she had, enjoy the privileges her two extra years granted her. I pretty much wanted to be her. I was thrilled when given clothes of hers which she'd outgrown. I was delighted Mum told her to let me join in her games.

Only gradually did I realise the adoration wasn't mutual. She'd say we were going to play hide and seek. "Count to one hundred and come and find me!"

I never could, not until it was nearly time to go back indoors. Then she'd tell me Mum wouldn't be pleased if I told her I got lost.

Lucinda was given a special doll for her birthday. Its eyes would open and close when it was laid down or lifted up, and it could talk. Inside the body was a device, which played back Mum and Dad's words wishing her a happy birthday.

Lucinda soon recorded over that. She let me listen, but I was never allowed to speak into the hidden microphone.

Over time the recorded words were replayed at a slower speed than the original and the sound became kind of echoey. Sometimes the doll told me I was a baby, or to go away. That was horrible, especially if no one else was in the room. Lucinda had discovered that if it was left switched on, but the 'play' button not pressed, it eventually spoke as though of its own accord.

Sometimes I woke in the night to hear it saying, "Come and find me." Lucinda had hidden it under my bed, outside the bedroom door, or in my wardrobe. Bleary eyed I'd stumble around the room, stubbing toes and banging shins until I located it. Then I recorded my own messages and drifted back to sleep with the doll whispering how nice I was. The mornings after it happened, Lucinda was praised for so generously sharing her favourite toy and Mum tucked an extra treat into her lunch box.

The odd thing was that Lucinda denied it. Of course she didn't let on to our parents that she was tormenting me, but she denied letting me borrow the doll too.

Mum just shrugged. "Maybe it can walk as well as talk?"

The last time I found the doll, it was resting on the collage I'd been doing for Mum. The paint was smudged and the paper flowers I'd spent ages cutting out neatly were crushed. I picked up the doll and marched towards Lucinda's room, then hesitated. When she was mean to me she went unpunished. If I told on her she'd twist it round somehow. The best thing to do was to copy exactly what she'd done to me. For that I had to know she was asleep before creeping into her room. To ensure I stayed awake myself, I waited in the bathroom. It was boring, so I opened the window in the hope of seeing a hedgehog or other creature of the night in the garden.

Lucinda's bedroom was next door and the bathroom window ledge wide enough for the doll. She'd never think of looking there!

I'm not sure if her yelp woke me, or if I hadn't got back to sleep by then. The latter I guess, as neither her faint cry, nor my giggles at the thought of her stubbing her toe and frustration at being beaten at her own game, woke our parents.

Mum's screams didn't wake me as I was already getting dressed by then. Usually I got out of bed at the last minute, but that morning I wanted to get to the bathroom before Lucinda. If she hadn't found the doll, I'd retrieve it and play the same trick again.

Following the noise I ran into my sister's bedroom. Mum turned from the window, pulled me close and told me not to look. I didn't close my eyes quickly enough and saw Lucinda's empty bed with the quilt thrown off.

There was a lot of activity after that. The ambulance and neighbours. Crying. I was hugged tight by grandparents, told not to worry. Lucinda was in hospital, but it didn't hurt, she was only sleeping.

Only gradually did I learn some of the truth. She'd fallen from her bedroom window, nobody knew how. Or why. The drop hadn't killed her, but she'd landed face down in a flower bed and couldn't breath in enough air.

"If only someone had found her sooner." A lot of people said that.

It wasn't until after her funeral I got upset. Yes she'd annoyed me sometimes, but I'd loved her. Without her lead to follow it seemed my future had somehow been taken away. I couldn't grow up to be just like her.

That night I heard, or thought I heard, the doll again. "Come and find me," it said in Lucinda's voice.

Where was it? I crept out and checked the bathroom window ledge. It wasn't there. Nor was it in the flower bed where my sister had fallen. As I let myself back indoors, Mum came down the stairs.

"What are you doing, Julie? What's happened to your feet?"

I tried to tell her I was looking for Lucinda's doll, but she'd smothered me in a hug before I got the last bit out.

"You miss her of course. We all do, love."

We walked up the stairs with her arm around me. At the top, I didn't turn towards my own room, but went straight ahead into my sister's. No one had been in there since the morning Mum looked out of the window. Lucinda's clothes were still on the chair where she'd bundled them before putting on her nightie. The quilt was still thrown back. The bed wasn't empty. It had been, I knew it had been, but I saw her doll right in the middle. It opened its eyes and said, "Come and find me."

I don't remember all of what came next. My terror resulted in me and Mum going to stay with my grandparents for a while. Dad phoned every night and came to visit at the weekends. When we went home, it was to the new bungalow, where they still live. No one mentioned Lucinda. There were no pictures of her, none of her clothes were passed on to me, none of my new teachers had taught her. It was as if she'd never existed… Until the dreams started.

For months I'd awoken most nights to hear my sister's

voice. "Come and find me," it said. Of course it was my imagination, but I didn't know what had triggered it. For years I'd rarely thought of Lucinda.

"Are you OK?" Mum asked.

"Yes," I said automatically. They'd spoken about Lucinda for the first time in something like fifteen years, maybe it wasn't a day to keep things hidden. "I've been having bad dreams. They started three months ago." I didn't need to ask if the date had any significance for them; I saw it in their faces.

"The storage company." Dad gestured to the bank statement as though I might have forgotten that the memories I'd hidden really were locked safely away somewhere. "They expanded and wrote to offer us a container in the new facility just up the road. We hadn't looked at her things since we put them there, so went along."

Mum had left the room by then. She was making tea, although we'd not finished the drinks we already had.

"What happened, Dad?"

"She had a talking doll that recorded…"

"I remember."

"Soon as we opened the crate, we heard our baby girl's voice ask us to find her."

I brought Mum back in and explained how the doll, if left switched on, would sometimes play messages unexpectedly. I told them about her leaving it to talk to me, but I made it seem like a fun game, not a mean trick to play on an adoring baby sister.

"After so long, wouldn't the battery be flat?" Dad asked.

"Not if it hasn't been in use. Remember how it opened its eyes when you picked it up? You must have set off that mechanism."

"Of course it must have been something like that," Mum said.

After that we moved on to sharing a few happy memories of Lucinda. She sounded such a sweet kid and tears fell as I thought of how much we'd all lost through her death.

"It doesn't seem right to leave her things shut up like that," Mum said.

That's when it hit me. I'd dreamed about Lucinda's doll as a kind of wake up call. Since my sister's death my parents had indulged me. They'd paid for everything I wanted and bought themselves a spoiled brat. It was time to stop being selfish. "I'll sort it out," I said.

There's a saying isn't there, something about fear itself being the only thing worth fearing? I was a bit nervous about seeing that doll again and knew I'd freak out if I too heard it speak the words Lucinda recorded so long ago. Even so I went straight over. Dad phoned the facility manager to explain and gave me his key, so I had no trouble gaining access.

It was fine. A bit emotional, looking at toys we'd squabbled over, the bright red coat I'd coveted and the, now silent, talking doll. I checked the battery compartment and found it empty. Dad must have done that when they came three months ago. The storage room was tiny, but even so the crate containing Lucinda's belongings didn't take up a large part of it. In less than half an hour I had everything sorted and in my car.

I took everything back to my parent's place, in case they wanted to check the things I'd earmarked for the charity shop. We spent a long time looking through photos, with my parents telling me who everyone was and trying to recall the various events. It was fun and I felt much closer to them than I had in a long time. Perhaps ever. I'd done the right thing at last and would sleep easily once again.

It was late and I was tired when I got home. I left the bags full of charity shop donations in the car and went straight to bed.

"Come and find me."

Did I dream that?

"Come and find me."

No dream. No confused memory. The sound is real.

I throw back my quilt and get out of bed. The voice is coming from outside. I follow it onto the balcony and look down. My car is below. In the back is the doll. There's no battery in it, yet still it speaks to me as loudly as though I was holding it close.

I wonder what Lucinda wants. Is it to apologise for tormenting me, or punish me for not finding her quickly enough? The tired, heavy feeling leaves my body and the breeze brushes through my hair. As I fall, I hear my sister call me one last time.

"Come and find me."

3. All Marjory's Girls

The tea was stewing in the pot, but Anna couldn't face returning to her mother's friends. Mum had only been gone two days and already they were bickering. No, worse than bickering; they were being downright nasty to each other and all under the pretence of honouring Mum's memory. Anna tried not to notice, but voices were growing louder.

"I"ll pay for a decent coffin and a good memorial stone."

"That's right, you've got the money so you call the shots!"

"We could each release a balloon. We did that when my little brother died and it was really moving."

"Balloons! You really think Marjory would have wanted to be remembered by us spreading litter across the countryside?"

"Oh give over you two. Yes, Marjory cared about the environment, but she wouldn't have tried to make someone feel guilty over the way they'd mourned a loved one."

"What about those lanterns then? It'd be beautiful if we did it at night and they burn away to nothing."

"Or set fire to the countryside. Anyway they have metal frames which kill wildlife and …"

"Stop it!" Anna yelled. "Have you forgotten her already? She'd have hated this. She's *my* mother. You pushed her away from me when she was alive, and when she lay dying, but you're not doing it now. Get out!"

They went, leaving Anna to weep alone. Mum would have

hated what she'd done even more than hearing the others argue. Anna had tried not to be jealous of them all, and eventually she'd pretty much succeeded. It had been difficult, especially at first. Anna's husband had left her when she'd discovered she couldn't have children. She'd turned to Mum for comfort and found she had to share it with half a dozen others.

After a while though, she started to see them not as rivals, but as friends. Each of them were suffering some kind of pain, and learning that helped her come to terms with her own. Under Mum's guidance it seemed they all became happier, better people. The women took the place of the sisters Anna never had and their children became her nieces and nephews. Anna recovered enough from her ex husband's rejection to risk looking again for love.

Henry was wonderful. The mirror showed she was middle aged and plain, but the woman reflected in his eyes was beautiful. She knew he'd never abandon her for something that wasn't her fault.

Mum was almost as keen as Anna. She baked Henry's favourite biscuits whenever there was a chance he might pop by. She wasn't so smitten she didn't take him to task over his hobby of keeping doves though.

"It's cruel to keep something wild in a cage. I've a good mind to come and let them out."

"They're not in cages, but a big run and they fly free all day. I only shut them in at night to keep them safe," Henry said.

"I should have known you weren't one to hurt something you love," Mum had said.

Henry was divorced, but stayed on good terms with his ex on account of their daughter. Lucy was a lovely girl; pretty, fun and full of passion. Mum had loved her as though she were a granddaughter and they'd gone on protests together as well as girly shopping trips. It seemed Anna would have her family after all – right until Lucy saw that's what she hoped for.

The girl had gone crazy, it seemed to Anna. She said awful things including suggesting Anna had split up her parents.

"I thought you were our friend, but I hate you!" she'd yelled and insisted her father choose between them.

Henry had suggested they see less of each other for a while until Lucy calmed down. "She'll come round," he'd said but Anna was too hurt to wait and ended the relationship completely.

Mum continued her friendship with Lucy, making Anna feel she'd taken her side.

"I'm not doing that," Mum had said. "How the girl treated you was wrong, but she's hurting too."

They'd not spoken of Lucy after that and Anna hadn't seen her.

Then Mum got frail. It seemed her ageing all happened at once and suddenly she really was the old lady her birth certificate claimed her to be. The doctor confirmed what Anna feared, Mum didn't have long left.

She came to stay with Anna. That's how they tried to think of it; as a visit. Anna once again began to resent the time and energy Mum spent on those other women. Mum was too weak to cope with more than one visitor at a time, so for hours on end Anna made tea and waited for her chance to sit with her own mother. Those others, the ones who were her friends too, weren't so bad. Maybe they even thought they were helping by giving her a break? Anna tried not to resent their presence, tried not to feel they were pushing in between her and Mum, edging her away.

She couldn't make that effort with Lucy. For Mum's sake she allowed the girl in and stayed polite, but she didn't pour her a cup of tea and didn't hug her and thank her for coming before she left.

Then Mum was gone. The women, her friends, came and spoke gently to Anna. They made her tea and ensured she ate. They didn't leave her alone. It had helped a little, until they gathered to arrange the funeral.

They'd all talked for a while about the songs they should play, the flowers they would order. Anna hadn't wanted to listen because she didn't want to accept Mum was dead and so these arrangements had to be made. Perhaps though Mum wasn't completely gone? Not if her friends were gathered together remembering her? That thought cheered her a little and she'd gone to fill the kettle. As it boiled the arguments started and Anna had sent them all away.

Anna sat with an untouched mug of stewed tea cold in front of her. Someone was knocking on the door and it seemed they weren't going away.

"Anna! Please let me in." It was Cara. The one who'd offered to pay for the coffin. The one who'd always been Anna's closest friend.

"I'm so sorry, Anna," she said as she opened the door. "We're all sorry. We said things we didn't mean. We're hurting, just like you."

Anna remembered words of her mother's about when people were grieving or angry or disappointed they sometimes hurt those closest to them. Mum had suggested forgiveness. Not always, not in the case of Anna's ex husband, but usually she considered that best. This was one of the cases where Anna agreed with her.

"I'm sorry too, Cara." The two women hugged.

"Silly thing is, we were doing it for you. Trying to, I mean. You generously shared your mother with us and we wanted to show we appreciated that."

"Yeah, I know. Come in and I'll make a fresh pot of tea."

"Tell us what you want done and allow us to help?" Cara pleaded when they both had a mug.

"What you all said about the flowers and the music, she'd have liked that. Not a fancy coffin and …"

"No. That was a silly idea. She told us she wanted a wicker one and for a tree to be planted over her. Something beautiful and living, not a great hunk of stone."

Anna nodded at words almost identical to Mum's own.

"It's just… I know you don't have a lot of money and I was trying to say that if there's anything you want it for …"

"Thanks, Cara. I can't think now. Let's try again tomorrow, shall we? Best behaviour all round?"

"OK. I, er …"

"What?"

"It's Lucy. She'd like to be involved too."

"I don't know if I can."

"There's something you don't know. It doesn't excuse all she said, but …"

Anna learned that, after winning a bitter and expensive custody battle, Lucy's mother had met someone and decided Lucy would be better off living with her father after all. When Henry told his daughter he wanted to marry Anna, he'd been unaware of his ex's decision and the fact she'd just explained it to Lucy.

"And Mum helped her deal with it. She would of course. Oh let the girl come, what difference does it make?" Anna said.

The following day, Lucy slipped past Anna with a whispered, "I'm so sorry."

There were no raised voices, just good suggestions.

"Cara has offered to pay for something to celebrate Mum's life. I think we should have a party. Not yet, I'm not ready yet. Let's just bury her quietly and meet up again in a month or so. Maybe we can laugh then about some of her antics. She'd have liked us to all be together, having fun."

They all agreed it was a good idea.

"I thought doves," Lucy murmured. "Instead of balloons we could release Dad's doves."

After an uncomfortable silence, Cara said, "I don't know if that'd be practical and I doubt your dad would be keen."

"I asked him. He said yes, if Anna would like it."

Anna could imagine the birds flying free, or appearing too. In reality they'd head straight back home so Henry could shut them in for the night. It would look lovely and would have pleased Mum. It was her this was all about, not Anna and not Lucy.

"Mum would have liked it. Thank him for me."

The service was beautiful. So many people shared happy memories of Mum. They sang her favourite songs and covered the simple wicker casket in the flowers she'd liked best. Anna cried all the way through, but the tears were cleansing ones. She said goodbye to most of the guests. Just those closest to Mum went to the graveside. As Mum's wicker coffin was lowered, Anna accepted the comfort of her friends. The friends Mum had made when she'd known, that when this time came, Anna would have no family by her side. There were no blood ties certainly, not a single one left, but she had these women, her chosen sisters.

Henry gently placed a dove in her hands, closing her fingers over its pure white wings so it sat calmly as he gave one to each of the others and then to his daughter. Anna released hers first. It flew straight into a tree where it sat watching her as, one by one, the others were set free.

Was it showing her that Mum was up there somewhere still looking after her? Or was it watching over the other birds, to be sure they were coming home too?

The next six birds rose high and flew away together. Then Lucy released hers. Another white one. It circled the tree as though urging Anna's to join it. As agreed, once their bird was gone, the women too went home. Anna remained alone.

"Goodbye, Mum," she whispered.

The dove flapped its wings and soared up and up and up.

As Anna turned to go she caught sight of Lucy and without thinking took a couple of steps toward her. "Why are you still here?"

"Sorry, I didn't mean for you to see me. I was just checking all the birds flew away."

"They've gone and all in the right direction." She paused. "It was the right thing to do. Thank you for suggesting it."

"Do you want to come and see if they're all back? Dad will be counting them in and I know he'd like to see you."

She knew what Mum would want her to say. That she'd want Anna to forgive, forget and start over. But Mum was gone now, she had to act for herself.

"Yes. Yes, I'd like that a lot."

4. Goodnight, Bert

An insistent, high-pitched scream echoed from the newly opened bookshop. Pulses of blue light sent eerie shadows hurtling down the High Street. Someone, or something, had triggered the alarm. Again.

In the safety of her car, Lauren took a few calming breaths. It was early and she was alone. Like any rational person she disliked leaving her warm bed on gloomy winter mornings – even more so at 3am. Once inside the newly opened bookshop she'd probably be confronted by mess and destruction. A burglar might be lurking.

None of that really worried her. What scared Lauren was finding the building empty, still securely locked, and no understandable accident to explain the alarm being set off. That could mean her business partner, Freya, was right. Their gorgeous new bookshop was haunted.

The landlord actually warned of the possibility when they first leased the place.

"When it was an art gallery, people sometimes felt a presence encouraging them to look at a certain picture. They spotted details they'd otherwise have missed that way. Things which made them smile or deal with real life situations. Like noticing flowers growing in a battle scene and then somehow seeing a ray of hope in their own bleak life," he said. "Rumour is that the ghost was a former caretaker, called Bert."

Lauren hadn't been the slightest bit bothered, because

back then she didn't believe in ghosts.

Freya, who did, was equally unconcerned. "An unpaid member of staff who'll be here twenty-four hours a day sounds like a bonus to me," she'd said.

The former art gallery, which closed while they were both still at school, had been popular and was missed by many local people. Lauren and Freya had chosen the name *Words As Art* for the bookshop partly to encourage an association with the former use of the property.

Nobody living ever objected to the girls using it for something else. Anything was better than seeing it empty and neglected over the last few years. The landlord apparently shared that view. He'd agreed a rent which was low enough that the two friends stood a chance of actually making a profit – provided there was no more mysterious damage.

There were some weird events as they'd decorated and put up shelving. Nothing major. They'd been working in the back office, at an early stage in the renovation, when they heard a doorbell ringing. A neighbouring shop manager had called to offer them his not very old till.

"The company are always modernising and updating. It's perfectly good, but destined for landfill, unless you'd like it?"

It wasn't until they'd assured him they would, and were exclaiming over that bit of good luck, they realised they couldn't have heard a door bell as they'd not yet fitted one.

Another day Lauren, standing on a stepladder, dropped the screwdriver. Almost immediately it reappeared in in her hand.

"Thanks, Freya," Lauren murmured.

"What did you say?" Freya called from the other side of the shop.

When Lauren explained, Freya said, "Thank Bert, our friendly poltergeist."

There were other similar little oddities, which Lauren felt would have a perfectly sensible explanation, if only she had time to think about it.

Although Lauren denied it, even to herself, there was a kind of atmosphere about the place. When she was there alone it hadn't felt lonely. It was as though she was wanted and welcomed. Just as though someone, something, was pleased she was there.

And then the first delivery of books had arrived.

The usually unflappable Freya seemed to panic at the thought of arranging them on the shelves. Lauren herself felt overwhelmed, but insisted it was just because this was all so new, and so important, to them both. They'd worked in bookshops before, but in well-established and ready-stocked places. Starting from scratch and having to make decisions on every little detail was naturally a bit daunting.

For the first time, since they'd become best friends in nursery school, Lauren and Freya rowed. They accused each other of shirking her share of the work, or undermining what the other had done.

"You might find it funny to put books about politics in the horror section, but we haven't got time to mess about," Freya snapped.

"Blaming me for your mistakes won't hide the fact you did practically nothing when I was at the dentist yesterday."

"Nothing? I …" she gestured to empty shelves. "But …"

Lauren expected to find the books her friend claimed she'd

unpacked, checked against the order, scanned for the barcode reader, and shelved, to still be in sealed boxes. They eventually discovered them jumbled together with packaging in the huge recycling bin. Even as she started to ask Freya why she'd done such a stupid thing Lauren realised she simply couldn't have. Freya loved books, they both had all their money and hopes invested in the business, and they'd never do anything to hurt the other. But if it wasn't either of them who was it?

That night Lauren received the first call from the alarm company. As it had been installed just a few days previously, and there was no money and few books in the store, she'd assumed it was a false alarm. She arrived to find a heavy, free-standing shelving unit had fallen, scattering books everywhere. She couldn't understand how that could have happened but, as there was no sign of forced entry, decided it was a freak accident.

The next night Lauren was called out again. Books had been pulled off shelves and hurled across the shop.

"No way could that be accidental," she told Freya the next morning.

"The poltergeist?" Freya suggested.

"Ghosts aren't real. There must be a rational explanation to this."

"It wasn't me, honestly," Freya said.

"Of course it wasn't. Why would you think I'd suspect you?"

"Other than the landlord, I'm the only one with a key."

"Can't see you walking three miles in the rain, sabotaging our efforts and disturbing my sleep just to convince me the place is haunted."

"I wouldn't do any of that… But that is the answer, I'm sure of it. The old caretaker from the art gallery is still here. To start with he was helping us, but now …"

"That makes no sense," Lauren said.

"I know. Why would he be angry?"

Lauren was still trying not to believe in book throwing ghosts, but didn't want to continue arguing with her friend. "Don't know, but clearly someone is. We need to start asking questions. You try people who remember the gallery. I'll go see our landlord."

That visit achieved just one thing, it ruled out their only, and unlikely, live suspect. Their landlord was cruising in the Caribbean so couldn't possibly have let himself into the shop.

Freya's research was more fruitful. She learned the alleged ghost was indeed named Bert, but hadn't been an official gallery employee. He was a homeless person who started coming in one winter, perhaps just to keep warm, and grew to love the paintings.

"Apparently he was unstable. Although usually gentle, when he was angry or frustrated he'd fly into a rage and cause damage. That's why he was unemployed and alone. The gallery owner must have felt sorry for him. Or maybe worked out there'd be less trouble if he was kept calm. Anyway, Bert was given small jobs to do in exchange for food and allowed to sleep there when the weather was bad. It became his only home."

As her friend spoke, Lauren had the weirdest feeling someone was listening to them. Someone who wanted answers and reassurance just as much as they did. "It can still be his home, can't it? Even when we open up?"

Freya looked startled. "You believe in him now then?"

"No. Don't know. Just thinking the idea through. If there really is a ghost who loved the gallery then he'd have been sad when it closed. Then, when we came along, he'd have thought it was opening up again and wanted to help out as he used to."

"Makes sense and that's how it felt. But why is he angry now?"

"It started when the books arrived. Maybe he realised it wasn't going to be a gallery and thought there'd no longer be a place for him?"

As they worked, Freya told the ghost that, as long as he didn't cause any more damage, he was welcome to stay. Lauren, feeling rather silly, joined in and explained how, just like paintings, books could bring people pleasure or help them.

For a while there were no more unexplained incidents, good or bad.

"Bert's gone," Freya said. "Maybe knowing it won't be a gallery again helped him move on?"

"There never was any ghost. They don't exist," Lauren said, although with far less conviction than in the past. She couldn't shake the idea they were both wrong.

That feeling was still with her when, a few nights after they'd opened, the security alarm was again triggered. Lauren drove along the deserted High Street. An insistent, high-pitched scream echoed from the bookshop. Pulses of blue light cast eerie, fleeting shadows. Someone or, more worrying, something, had triggered the alarm. Again.

In the safety of her car, she took a few calming breaths. As previously, there was no sign of a break-in and the shop was still properly locked. Lauren hastily silenced the alarm. The sudden quiet was full of anger. Lauren didn't really want to switch on the light, but knew she must.

There wasn't much damage, just a few books tossed around and their careful display of leaflets and bookmarks swept onto the floor. It wouldn't take long to tidy up, but that wasn't the point. Lauren's fears were confirmed; Bert was real and he was angry.

Lauren admitted to her friend that she now believed in the existence of this particular poltergeist. "Go on, say you told me so!"

Freya shook her head. "I'd rather you were wrong. I've always believed in ghosts and wanted to meet one – but the reality isn't what I hoped. To me ghosts are people who want to stay in touch with loved ones. Or who've come to comfort us, or maybe are still here because they have unfinished business. I've never thought of them as wanting to hurt people who've never done anything bad to them and I can't see how we've done that."

"Not on purpose anyway. Maybe we've done it accidentally? Our landlord must be due back from his cruise soon. I'll email asking for any information he has about the unofficial caretaker."

"We do know he didn't have any money. Maybe he's angry we're selling the books, rather than making them available for free?" Freya suggested.

"Could be. Expect he'd prefer a library here."

"I'd really like to make him happy, but we have a living to make."

"Perhaps there are things we can do to make books more accessible to people who can't afford many new ones?"

Lauren said. They did hope to earn their living from *Words As Art*, but it wasn't their only reason for opening the bookshop. They both wanted to share their passion for books with those who already loved the written word, and bring that joy to new readers.

The girls set up a reading corner with comfy sofas and free drinking water. They invited people to sit and read for as long as they wanted, provided they were careful with the books. In addition they offered secondhand books for as low a price as they could manage. The new area was in use for less than two days before there were problems.

Readers rarely stayed long. Lauren overheard more than one saying they didn't feel welcome. The water cooler fell several times, despite nobody having knocked it. It either soaked the sofas, or the contents shot out at improbable angles, drenching readers and nearby stock. Clearly the ghost was still angry, but they couldn't work out why.

Their landlord called in soon after. "I got your email while I was in Guadalupe and gave it some thought in between cocktails," he said. "I felt sure that somewhere amongst the old deeds and things I'd seen some actual facts about him. When I got back, I dug out a kind of tenancy agreement with a man identified simply as Bert. It fits in time-wise with the rumours about the ghost's origins."

"So he had a right to consider this shop his home?" Freya asked.

"I don't think it would have had any legal standing. Here, you have a look."

The agreement was that Bert could live in the gallery, provided he caused no damage and did nothing to upset those who came to view, and possibly buy, the paintings. There was a statement saying the terms had been explained to him. It was signed by the building's owner, the chap who ran the gallery, and had an X under Bert's name.

"It seems to me it was just something to reassure him and keep him in order," their landlord said.

Freya nodded. "And it's just about the gallery. Once our books arrived and Bert realised things had changed, he didn't feel bound by it. Thanks for showing us, but I don't think it helps."

"I do," Lauren said. "This was read to him, and he signed with an X. Bet he couldn't read. Just imagine how frustrating it would be to spend all your time surrounded by books, knowing readers were entertained for hours, seeing them laugh, or cry, and yet the words meant nothing to you."

"I'd want to throw one then," Freya admitted.

"Exactly. And remember he calmed down when we explained how they were like the paintings? He was waiting, hoping he'd come to love them."

"Don't you have any books with pictures in?' the landlord asked.

Lauren showed, and sold, him a beautifully illustrated guide to the Caribbean, and then thanked him for coming by.

"I'm not sure more picture books are really the answer," Freya said once he'd left.

"Me neither. What we're going to do is teach Bert to read."

Freya laughed.

"I'm serious."

"A few weeks ago you didn't believe in ghosts. Now you've met one who's known to get frustrated easily, hates books, shows it by hurling them around with what looks like a great deal of force, and you're going to sit him down and teach him to read?"

"Yes. Sort of. I'll think of something."

It didn't take Lauren long to come up with a plan. The library started running free adult literacy classes. All kinds of people came. Rich and poor, youngish and not young at all. There were those who'd not received much education for varying reasons. Some for whom English wasn't their first language. Several elderly people who Lauren was sure could read perfectly well but were in serious need of company. And a man who'd lost his sight and enjoyed listening as others read.

The classes were a great success. Those who could afford to bought books – and brought in cakes and other snacks, which they shared with everyone. Friendships were made, some prejudices overcome, and the love of reading shared.

There were no more unexplained accidents, or late night call-outs by the security firm. Nothing at all really to suggest their poltergeist was still with them. Even so Lauren and Freya were both convinced Bert listened in at every class, and a couple of people remarked how sometimes they'd almost hear a gentle voice sounding out the letters with them. Later, others said whenever they picked up a book they'd been practising on, it always seemed to fall open at the right page.

It was a long time before Lauren again drove down the High Street in the early hours of the morning. She was returning from the wedding of two of her literacy class members. Appropriately they'd both given readings – and done so flawlessly. Lauren had been very pleased to witness that, even though she'd been certain they could read long before she met them. She'd been delighted too to receive the large order of books as wedding favours. How nice the couple chose to share their love of books as they demonstrated their love for each other.

As she neared *Words As Art*, Lauren saw a light. For a moment she worried it was the alarm, but almost instantly realised it was a faint, steady glow coming from inside, not a bright flashing beam from the box above the door. Had it not been her shop she probably wouldn't have noticed it at all.

She parked outside the bookshop, quietly let herself in and disabled the alarm. The light shone from a lamp in the reading area. It was angled to illuminate one end of the squashiest of the comfy sofas, but not light up the surrounding area. The sofa had an indent, just as though something she couldn't see was sitting there. On the arm of the sofa was a book. A slip of paper marked Bert's place in the latest history of art the shop had acquired.

Lauren let out a calm breath and smiled. This was the ghostly equivalent of reading by torchlight under the sheets. She whispered "Goodnight, Bert," and went home to her nice warm bed.

5. Very Ordinary Vase

"You're not superstitious are you, Claire?" Rose asked. She sounded just as awkward as she had when she'd asked after John.

It was an odd thing for her to ask me, but everything about her visit so far had been a bit odd. Only a little bit and in a good way really, but I was feeling slightly unsettled.

"Of course not, you know that," I replied, trying to sound convincing. Actually I'd had to try the same thing when I'd told her everything with John was fine.

"That's OK then." She settled back onto my smokey grey-blue cushions and sipped her coffee. She looked good, better than she had for months. Getting made redundant totally knocked her confidence and she'd sort of shrunk away to nothing. Not physically I don't mean. Actually she'd gained a bit of weight, though looking at her then it seemed she'd started to lose it. The main difference though was that her confidence had returned.

Rose seemed so much like her old self I assumed she'd come to tell me she'd got another job. I was so sure I actually asked, "How's the job hunting going?"

"Pretty good. I've had a couple of interviews. Not heard back yet, so there's still hope and I've got anther one next week I'm really hopeful about."

"Excellent!"

I was wary though. She's been applying for jobs for

months with no luck and I worried this was a case of getting her hopes up only to have them dashed all over again.

"Isn't it? I think volunteering in the charity shop has something to do with it. Sounds better than saying I'm doing nothing and it's a lot better for me than watching daytime TV and eating biscuits."

"Yes, that's true."

"And I've picked up a few bargains. I got myself a smart interview suit for peanuts and a few things for the flat, which reminds me …"

Uh oh, here it came. I'd been half expecting her to ask for a loan for some time. And dreading it since the idea first crossed my mind. It's not that I didn't want to help out a friend, but I didn't have much spare cash myself and I knew from experience that loans to friends could cause bad feeling.

"I've got you a present," Rose said and handed me something wrapped in tissue paper. "To be honest I bought it for myself. I thought it would look perfect on my mantlepiece."

I unwrapped the package to reveal a smokey grey-blue vase. A rather beautiful vase. "It's lovely." Reluctantly I handed it back. "But you should keep it. It's the perfect match for your Gran's candlestick."

"That's what I thought, but it isn't. It just looks wrong somehow. Then I remembered these cushions." She patted one. "And I thought it'd look perfect here."

"It will, thank you."

When she was ready to leave, I thanked her again and wished her good luck with the interview.

"It'll be fine, touch wood." She crossed her fingers and

tapped them against my doorframe. "And remember, no getting superstitious!"

I tried the vase in a few different places, trying to decide on the perfect spot. It looked good just about anywhere, but deserved the perfect setting. The first time it wasn't where I thought I put it, I just assumed I'd moved it again without really thinking. The second time I guessed John had moved it.

"Why would I?" he'd asked.

Good question. He wasn't ever there long enough to bother about my interior decor. He arrived in time to eat the nice dinner I cooked him, drink the nice wine I'd bought, and go to bed. In the morning he'd eat the breakfast I got up early to make and leave before his coffee cup had cooled.

"Don't know what you want it for anyway," he said.

"To put flowers in?"

"You know I'm not into all that nonsense."

I did. John didn't buy me flowers, or take me out, or waste his money on a surprise box of chocolates. He didn't waste my money on those things either. He'd borrowed 'a few quid just to tide me over' on numerous occasions. He'd paid maybe a quarter of it back. I tried not to remember how much he might still owe, it just caused bad feeling. I certainly didn't mention it.

Of course he was using me in a way. I did see that. But wasn't I doing the same? I was desperate for company and affection and if I didn't have John visiting once a fortnight or so, I wouldn't have anyone. That became a catch 22. I was reluctant to commit to social functions in case John decided to visit the same day.

"You realise he could be married?" Rose had said.

"Doubt it. Why would anyone who had a wife be interested in me?"

"Because you're fun, kind, intelligent and pretty?"

"You're just saying that because you're my friend."

"If John's not saying those things, maybe he isn't?"

After that we hadn't discussed him much.

I quickly washed the frying pan, John's ketchup smeared greasy plate and my own muesli bowl, and set off for work.

Mostly it was a good day until someone showed us the cute little booties she'd bought for the baby her sister was expecting. Sally sobbed. Sally is never exactly happy, but anything to do with babies makes the situation much worse. I wheeled her chair out the office and down the corridor, then I hugged her until she was just quietly sniffing.

"My period started this morning," she said eventually.

"That often makes people emotional," I told her. "What you need is tea and first dibs in the biscuit barrel."

Obviously that wasn't the solution to her problem, but it got her calm and heading back to her desk.

"Time of the month," I stage whispered as we returned with the tea tray.

The others offered paracetamol and advised she try a hot water bottle that evening as though they'd not noticed her meltdown. Sympathy over Sally's real problem just embarrasses her and there's nothing we can do to help.

I stopped at the supermarket on my way home as I always did after one of John's visits. Not being a big meat eater myself means I have to make a point of restocking things like bacon, sausages and steaks once he's been round. Really it would make more sense to wait a week, so there's less risk of it going to waste, but one time I was caught out with nothing other than a prawn salad to offer for his dinner and cereal for his breakfast. He hadn't been happy.

When I got in, the vase had moved again. I knew it had because just as I'd been about to leave that morning I'd spotted a greasy mark on it. After I'd wiped it clean, I'd taken care to place it right in the centre of the coffee table. After work it was on the shelf in the hallway. If I didn't live alone, the shelf wouldn't be visible, but with just my couple of coats hanging above it, the vase was easy to spot. Years ago, in the playground at school, Rose had once shoved a snowball down my back. I felt that icy sensation again just then. Something wasn't right.

Touching the doors as little as possible I looked into each room. No signs of any disturbance or anything missing, so the vase hadn't been moved by a burglar who'd been interrupted. Nothing else was ever out of place and I'd not felt any kind of 'presence' so the flat wasn't haunted by a poltergeist. I laughed at myself then. I don't believe in such things and I'd assured Rose I wasn't superstitious.

Of course that was it. Her keep asking that had put ideas into my head. I was feeling a bit fed up with John that morning. The hallway was so bare because there wasn't a jacket of his hanging there. He didn't leave so much as a toothbrush in the bathroom. Other than when he was eating my food or sleeping in my bed there was no sign at all that he was part of my life. To be honest he wasn't part of my life at all. I'd never met any of his family, he'd not met mine, we didn't share anything. I must have been thinking something like that rather than concentrating on where I placed the vase and accidentally carried it out into the hall.

As I ate my tea I stared at the vase. It still looked wrong. Not, I realised, because of the location but because it was empty. On Friday I bought myself a spray of carnations. The vase looked even better holding flowers and because it was full I didn't absent mindedly move it and scare myself silly. On Sunday I cooked myself a mixed grill. I didn't want all that meat going to waste and since I'd met John I'd got used to eating more of it. The meal was OK, but I didn't really enjoy it. It was food I'd grown accustomed to, but I'd have enjoyed eggs Florentine or al dente pasta with a generous scoop of pesto and sprinkling of parmesan far more.

Carnations last a long time, but mine were looking less than pristine when I next had a visit from John. I saw him notice them, but he didn't say anything. After he'd gone I decided they looked terrible and chucked them out. I soon had the flat clean and tidy again, but I felt somehow dissatisfied. More flowers, that's what I needed. I bought some after work. Not from the supermarket as I didn't bother going there. Instead I made a mad sprint for the florist, arriving as the lady was bringing in buckets of blooms.

"Take your time," she said. "I'm never in a rush on Tuesdays."

As I made my selection she told me she held flower arranging classes on Tuesday evenings. As she chatted I had a mental picture of my smokey blue-grey vase holding a tasteful arrangement, not a few cheap blooms plonked in any old how. That's what it deserved, but of course I couldn't sign up for a course. John might call when I was out.

The freesias I decided on smelled wonderful and looked just right. At least I thought so.

"They make me sneeze," John said three days later, although he hadn't sneezed at all. "What's for dinner?"

"I haven't got anything much in. Why don't we go out for a change?"

He hadn't wanted to and grudgingly agreed to a takeaway after I made it clear it was that or share the salad I'd planned to eat myself. Ordering the food did make a change, but I still paid for, served, ate and cleared up after a meal I hadn't wanted. That was something I'd become accustomed to.

The next time John visited, the vase held roses in the softest shade of pink. He glared at them.

I looked from his disapproving face to the flowers. They looked nice enough, but properly arranged with some greenery and maybe a few pieces of gypsophila they could look magnificent and would be a credit to my gorgeous vase.

I started trying to explain to John that he couldn't just turn up unannounced on Tuesdays any longer as, if he wasn't coming, I'd be at flower arranging classes. Somehow though I only got the first bit out before he demanded to know if it was something to do with whoever was giving me flowers.

"Yes, I suppose it is."

He was gone before he even learned I still hadn't bought steak. He did come back; on Tuesday. He left a note which started off with him sounding annoyed. I don't know how it finished because I didn't read it all. There wasn't time after my flower arranging class. I had to quickly get ready to meet Rose; she'd just started a new job and we were going out to celebrate.

Maybe I got a bit obsessed with the flower arranging, but it was a harmless entertainment and, without John to shop for, one I could easily afford. I bought more vases and often had an arrangement on my desk at work as well as several at home. I got pretty good at getting them how I wanted and choosing flowers to set off the containers. The old grey vase started to let the side down a bit. The smokey colour was sort of depressing and it looked odd in the living room as it almost, but not quite, matched my gorgeous blue-grey cushions. I put it in the cupboard under the sink which is where it stayed until Allan, my new boyfriend, took me to meet his brother.

"Umm, just don't mention babies," he whispered as he rang the doorbell.

When Sally answered I immediately understood why not. She was as surprised as I was to discover my boyfriend was the brother of her husband. It was still early days in our relationship so I'd not said much about him at work and Sally hadn't been saying much about anything for a while. While I was there she made a real effort to be cheerful, but I could see it was an act.

The next day as I was leaving for work, I noticed the grey vase on the hallway shelf. It didn't get there by itself; vases just don't do that. Since I'd met Allan I was sometimes a bit distracted, a bit daydreamy and he'd brought me flowers when he picked me up to visit Sally and her husband. Quite likely I'd got the vase out without paying attention to what I was doing. It wasn't a sign of anything; I'm not superstitious. My life was much better than it had been before I'd got the vase, but not because it had any weird powers or anything.

I took the newspaper from the recycling bin, wrapped the vase and took it into work.

"Sally, are you superstitious?" I asked in a quiet moment. Maybe not the best thing to ask a woman who has every right to feel unlucky, but it had to be done.

"Not really, but to be honest if anyone told me eating four leaved clover would make me pregnant I'd mow the lawn for my tea."

"This is absolutely nothing like that at all." I handed her the vase. "I just noticed that you put the flowers Allan gave you into a yellow vase which doesn't go with your pink walls at all and thought this would look much better."

"Oh, Claire it's lovely, thank you!"

The vase made no difference to her life. Sally didn't get pregnant. She didn't even continue with the IVF. Instead she and her husband have adopted a five-year-old girl. Sally is happier than I've ever known her.

"Claire, I have a confession to make… About the vase," she confided on my hen night. "I've given it to my neighbour. She's not been well and needed cheering up. You're not upset are you?"

"No, not as long as you haven't promised it'll help her."

"Don't worry, I haven't and anyway, she's definitely not superstitious; I asked her. Twice.

6. The Digressions Of Will

Hi, I'm William Wastenot, a particularly fine example of *Rattus rattus* if I do say so myself. I can tell we're going to be friends, so you can call me Will.

You humans don't usually seem that fond of rats. Can't think why, especially when I see my reflection in a puddle. I'm all cute and furry with gorgeous yellow teeth, lovely long, worm-like tail and bright, beady eyes. What's not to love? There's my feet too. Nice scrabbly feet with long toes and the cutest little claws. But I digress.

Waste, that's what I wanted to talk about. I hate waste. We all do, don't we? In these times of recession and ecological responsibility, even humans realise they shouldn't just chuck away stuff if it's perfectly useful to someone, somewhere. What's that look for? Worried about the pizza crusts you didn't finish last night or the just past its sell-by date cheese you found in the fridge this morning? Wondering if you put them somewhere a rat could get them? Worry no more. You did. Deeelish!

That's what I mean by teamwork. Oh, didn't I get to that bit yet? Me and my ratty mates make a good team. We discover where food's regularly available and we tell everyone; even scabby Uncle Walter. Disgrace he is.

"Just 'cos you got a few fleas and a bit of mange, there's no need to let yourself go," I told him. Doesn't listen though, except when I mention food.

I mention it a lot (you may have noticed). Well, it's

important to rats. We like getting together over a good meal. Invite one of us round and pretty soon you've got the whole family and a party going on. Ah, I can tell by your face you didn't think you'd invited me. 'Course you did. Everything from chips dropped in the street to old sofas thrown over a hedge are an invitation to rats.

But I digress. Again. Waste, that's what I wanted to talk about. Not much gets wasted around here. You chuck it out and us rats eat it or live in it or bury our dead in it. Teamwork that is – and recycling. All good stuff. At least, that seems the proper way to do things to right-minded people like us. Your neighbours might disagree.

D'you know, some people are so mean they only buy the food they're going to eat and don't give a thought to supplying me and the other rats? Their old furniture doesn't become a cosy roadside refuge for my cousins, but is sold or given to other humans to go in their houses. Even what's obviously proper rubbish and should go to holiday parks, doesn't. Oh! Better explain that. Your landfill tips are our holiday parks. Luverly places they are. All that nicely rancid food, slime underfoot and wonderful fragrance get us all romantic, so there's soon baby rats, if you catch my drift. Me and my girl we often…

Oops, digressing again. The problem with waste, that's my point. Stupid bigwig human mayors and governors and the like, who should mind their own business getting drunk in clubs and chatting up Russian spies, decided there was too much going into landfill. How daft can you get? Can't have too much of a good thing. I was soon proved right. People sorted the things they threw out. Plastic, glass, paper and the like went off to be made into more plastic, paper and glass stuff. Much less extra food was bought – and some of the spare was given to other humans who couldn't afford any. Crazy idea. Rats started to starve. Soon there weren't so many of us. To save poor old Will (that's me – you have been paying attention haven't you and not just thinking about getting yourself a sandwich, haven't you?) I got myself down the docks.

There's always been rats down the docks. Some of my ancestors, poor things, was on the Titanic. Others were on the QE2. Oh what a ship that was, I'm told. Thinking about that gave me my idea. There's luverly grub on cruise ships. Lots and lots and lots of it. Sponge cakes and steaks, lamb and ham, cream teas and cheese. Just thinking about it makes me come over all poetic.

Decided to stow away, didn't I? It was scare-eeeee. First was the most dangerous bit. I had to get on the trash barge. That's the little boaty thing that takes rubbish off the ships over to the incinerator. Getting on that was dead easy. I just waited until it was tied up and nipped up the rope. These scrabbily feet don't just look pretty you know. It was easy as I say, but scary too and nearly my downfall.

Oh, the food that was on there! The cheese. Huge great wedges of the very best cheese. I took a bite and then another. All that gorgeous grub and other useful stuff just going to be burned. A crime it was, so I was doing my best to save as much cheese as possible. By save, I mean eat, of course. *This* close to being incinerated I was. Just escaped by the scales on my tail!

Got on the cruise ship eventually, I did. Wasn't so easy that bit. The way these cruise companies carry on it's as though they don't want rats helping them with their waste problem. Getting on was tricky, staying on looked impossible. Hygiene measures! I won't go into details as this ain't a horror story. All I'll say is it's health and safety gone mad. So I jumped ship onto a yacht and made my way home.

Were my humans glad to see me? Nope. They've gone green. Sounds good, I know. Kind to wildlife, you'd think. Maybe, but not rats as it turns out. Don't leave me so much as a crumb so I've had to move out.

At last, I've got to the point of the story – and it's the absolute best bit. I've looked in your bins. You don't faff about separating your rubbish, making sure your bins always go out on time, or reducing food waste. That shows me we'll make a great team. So I'm moving in with you. How great is that? While you're jumping around and squealing with excitement at the sight of me, I'll just nip out and fetch the family.

7. Unforgettable Flowers

As the train came into the station, Joshua's phone beeped. Without looking, he knew the message said 'you have the car!' He'd set up the reminder that morning, just in case he forgot Chloe hadn't dropped him off as usual and therefore wouldn't be collecting him.

"I'm not working today," she'd reminded him over breakfast. "I'm having my hair done and then making beef Wellington for dinner, so try not to be late home."

Joshua was pleased with himself for not having forgotten about the car and so wasted time waiting for his wife. Beef Wellington was his absolute favourite. Both he and Chloe would have been disappointed if he'd caused it to be spoiled. Using the calender reminder function on his phone was a brilliant idea. His sister, who'd often rescued him from his own forgetfulness, would have been impressed.

"Honestly, Josh, you couldn't be more of a stereotypical nutty professor if you tried," Louise had claimed when he'd called to wish her, rather than his wife, many happy returns on Chloe's birthday one year.

"I'm not nutty, just… Oh, what's the word?"

She'd known he was teasing. Bad as his memory was, it was good enough for him to remember his tendency to be absent minded. Remembering Louise was hard for a different reason: she was no longer with them.

Joshua let himself into the house and called out, "I'm

home, Chloe love."

As she kissed him, Joshua was aware something was different. She smelled of… Oh, hairspray! She'd been to the salon.

"Your hair looks nice," he said.

"Thank you." She kissed him again.

The dining table looked good too. She'd put out their best glasses, and candles. Joshua could have kicked himself for feeling smug about remembering the message he'd set about the car. If he hadn't, he'd have looked at the calender feature again and perhaps realised, before reaching home, that it was their wedding anniversary.

Joshua had absolutely no excuse not to remember. Chloe's comments that morning were hints and it wasn't as though his university schedule had been more hectic than usual. He could easily have bought her a gift at lunchtime or even picked something up on the way home. He'd done that several times before. His sister had saved the day more than once by texting him and asking him to stop by her florist shop on the way home.

"Freesias are Chloe's favourite," she'd said as she made up a birthday or anniversary bouquet. Louise had known that as she'd arranged all their wedding flowers, and unlike her brother had possessed an excellent memory.

"Gerberas are mine," she'd told him. "So bright and cheerful. Make sure there are lots at my funeral."

Joshua hadn't liked her talking about her illness, but she'd been right to do so. It had comforted him, when the time came, to know he'd followed her wishes – even if it had been Chloe who'd reminded him exactly what they were.

It wasn't that he was uncaring, just that details often

escaped him. He'd often bought Chloe or Louise a little gift if he happened to spot something they might like, then not think to do that when they needed cheering up or it was a special occasion. Twice he'd asked Louise to create a bouquet for Chloe, who'd laughed and reminded him they were going on holiday the next day.

Joshua could still recall how he'd felt at their wedding and never forgot that he loved his wife, he just didn't always realise the date or associate it with the event. What made forgetting their anniversary somehow worse was that he knew she'd totally understand.

Even so, he apologised. "I should have booked a table or cooked your dinner."

"It's your anniversary too, so it's right I do something for you," Chloe said.

"I'm so lucky to have you and I'll try really hard to remember next year."

Chloe chuckled. "Your memory is even worse than I realised! Look at that." She indicated a huge bouquet.

He hadn't bought them, he was positive. Yes, he was capable of forgetting he'd placed an order, but it would have come back to him now he'd been prompted.

"You even made sure it has my favourites."

"Freesias," he said, inhaling the sweet scent. There were other blooms too, all in soft pink and champagne shades. Roses and carnations he recognised. Amongst them were some which although he associated with brighter colours, he knew must be gerberas; his sister's favourites.

8. Voodoo Val

The sudden appearance of the boss, right next to her desk, made Val jump. Again.

"What is going on here?" Shirley demanded.

As what was 'going on' was that her entire staff were sticking pins into a drawing of Shirley, there wasn't a rush of explanations. There were however a few nervous glances in Val's direction. Understandably so, as it was she who'd drawn the cartoon and invited her colleagues to vent their frustrations with pins, hole punches and highlighter pens.

Val felt both hot and cold at the same time. Could she get the sack for this? Although the job had lost much of its appeal, Val didn't want, and couldn't afford, to lose it.

She said, "I'm responsible. May I speak to you privately?" Maybe she could ensure no one else got into trouble with her.

Shirley nodded and strode off to her office. The other staff started speaking, a few rose from their seats, but Val waved them back down.

"Don't worry, I'll talk to her and sort it out," she said.

Val tried to make her voice confident and her smile optimistic, but didn't feel either of those things. Shirley's reaction would be unpleasant at best, but it was herself she was annoyed at. Why on earth had she taken such a stupid risk? Earlier that same day Shirley had suddenly appeared in the office, making Val jump and catching the staff out.

"Gosh, eleven o'clock already, is it?" Shirley had said in mock surprise.

The expressions on the faces of her staff had been the genuine article; they wouldn't have made their coffee ten minutes early, nor been laughing over their horoscopes in the paper, if they'd thought she'd be back in time to witness it.

"Near enough," Tanya had said.

"My watch must be slow," Shirley replied, as though she thought she was being hilariously amusing. She sauntered off towards her own office.

"Usually is at home time," Tanya muttered.

"Shh, she'll hear you," Julia cautioned.

"Don't care if she does. She's a sarcastic cow."

Personally Val agreed both that it would be better to keep your voice down when criticising the new boss and that Shirley was indeed sarcastic, but didn't say so. Instead she sketched a quick, unflattering cartoon of Shirley and stuck her tongue out at it. Very childish, but it made her feel slightly better. She ripped it up and threw it in the bin.

The women were all squabbling, so didn't notice. Some blamed Tanya for getting them into trouble; as well as being the most outspoken, it had been her idea to put the kettle on. Others said 'someone' should have pointed out there was no written rule about when they took their breaks.

Soon the bickering subsided into a tense silence. Val sighed. Since Shirley had replaced their old boss, Angie, all the staff were irritable with each other. Harpers Accounting used to be a really fun place to work and they'd got everything done, despite the odd moments of silliness. Now they were miserable and unable to keep up with the workload.

Angie's door had always been open, literally and figuratively. Angie couldn't solve every work or personal problem, but even if she couldn't, she'd listen sympathetically and let the person know she was on their side. As a result, the staff were always ready to do that bit extra, when Angie needed them too.

Once, when Easter coincided with the end of the tax year, they'd all agreed to work on a bank holiday and take a day off another time. At coffee time they'd heard the chimes of an ice cream van.

"Can we go and get one, so we don't feel we're totally missing out on our day at the seaside?" Tanya had asked.

Angie laughed. "Go on then."

When everyone came back with their 99s and strawberry mivvies, they discovered Angie had pushed all their seats into a double row. Angie sat at the front, pretending to be the driver on a coach trip. They'd all laughed as though it was the funniest thing they'd ever done as they sang *'We Do Like To Be Beside The Seaside'* and *'Day Trip To Bangor'*. It hadn't taken up much more time than a normal tea break but two years later it was still talked about fondly.

Val knew they'd miss Angie after she retired. Everyone said Val should have her job, but Val didn't apply. She loved being part of a happy team, but didn't want to lead it. She'd be fine at the cajoling and rewarding parts, but wouldn't know what to do if that didn't work.

At first Shirley seemed OK. No one had felt able to pop into her office to talk over problems, but she kept the door physically open. She never joined the others for tea break chats, but did get their old kettle replaced when she ordered one for her own office. Shirley completed her own work efficiently, but that was kind of the problem. She was rigid about what was and wasn't her job and had no interest in teamwork or flexibility.

When two people wanted the same week off work, Shirley signed the form of the most senior employee and returned the other with 'denied' written across it in red ink. It was company policy that senior staff had first choice over holiday periods, but the red pen was entirely Shirley's invention.

Val had quietly explained, "Angie would have asked them to see if they could work it out between them."

"And whenever I'm given requests for time off, I'll deal with them according to company policy. Now, are you going to give me another history lesson, or actually do some work?"

Val was hurt; all she'd intended was to help everyone concerned. If Shirley could only learn to be more like Angie, life would be easier for them all. However, rather than mellowing, Shirley had gone from unfriendly to downright nasty.

Not long afterwards, Julia asked if she could start later in the mornings and stay later to make up the time.

"Working hours are nine to five-thirty," was Shirley's immediate response.

Val tried to talk her round.

"Let me guess, Angie would have said yes?" Shirley practically sneered.

"Maybe, maybe not, but she wouldn't have made a decision without asking why the request was made."

"In case you haven't yet worked it out, I'm not Angie."

"I know that."

"And do you also know what hours you're all contracted to work? It shouldn't be difficult to remember as you were reminded less than a month ago."

Shirley was right. New contracts had been brought in just after Shirley started. Several people's job descriptions had been changed with a 'take it or leave' attitude from head office.

"Quit grumbling and be grateful you're not in my shoes," she'd snapped when Tanya suggested a pay rise should accompany the new contracts. Actually, since then she snapped at nearly everything.

If anyone arrived even a minute late, they'd be called into her office and given an unnecessarily loud official warning. At five twenty-nine she'd walk round the office, checking no one had been tempted to switch off their computer a moment too soon. Stationery supplies had to be signed for and written requests put in for medical or dental appointments, including a signed statement that it hadn't been possible to arrange this outside working hours.

Shirley's attitude had rubbed off on everyone to some extent. People snapped at each other if someone borrowed a pen without asking, and refused to help out if something wasn't strictly their job. Slowly everyone was becoming a little less happy. Many of them had looked for other jobs; the lack of these making them feel trapped. The number of days people called in sick had increased. Even when staff were present, stress meant work suffered, which didn't please Shirley, who became more irritated and demanding. It was a vicious circle.

Val decided they needed to do something to release the tension or life would be unbearable for everyone. At lunchtime she drew the cartoon of Shirley and invited everyone to stick in pins. A few people made half-hearted attempts, which they giggled at. Julia reached over to have a try and realised she was holding a paperclip, not a pin. Everyone joined in her laughter.

One girl's mascara ran, giving her face a weirdly comic look. Soon they were all laughing almost uncontrollably. If anyone stopped, the sight of the others chortling away set them off again. It wasn't that the situation was especially funny, Val realised. It was more that they were happy to all be on the same side again.

That was until Shirley had appeared. Val had tried to warn the others by hissing, "It's Shirley."

"I know and her hair's all curly," Julia answered, pointing to the damage she'd done to the top of Val's drawing with a hole punch. That set everyone off again.

"What is going on here?" Shirley demanded, causing them to shut up immediately.

Val admitted responsibility and trailed Shirley to her office. Her face felt like it was burning, and her stomach as though she'd swallowed a huge chunk of ice.

As soon as they reached Shirley's office, she gestured to the sheet of paper Val hadn't realised she'd snatched up. "What is that?"

Val, her hand shaking slightly, showed her.

"It's supposed to be me?"

Val nodded.

"And you've all attacked it like some kind of voodoo doll?" The quiet calm of Shirley's voice was completely unnerving.

"No! Well sort of, but it's not like we mean you any real harm!" Suddenly she realised how horrible that must seem to

Shirley. "I'm so sorry. We don't mean you any harm at all, we're just… On edge, unhappy. I just meant it as a joke to help everyone let off steam and bind us together …"

"Over a common enemy?"

"Sort of, I suppose. But we don't want an enemy." Before she lost her nerve entirely, she explained how uptight everyone was and how they, and the work, was suffering as a result.

"And you feel that's my fault?" Shirley didn't sound angry. In fact for once she seemed to be interested in what Val had to say.

Why not be honest? "Frankly, yes. You're so rigid that it's making us the same way, with work, you, and each other."

"Unlike Angie?"

"Well… Yes."

"You do realise she wasn't forced to retire? I didn't push her out, just applied for the post after she'd made her decision."

Val nodded. She had known that, but still blamed Shirley for taking Angie's place. That wasn't exactly fair.

"I'm fully aware how wonderful Angie was and that I don't measure up. You've all made that perfectly clear."

To Val's horror, she saw Shirley was on the verge of tears. Without thinking, she reached across and squeezed her boss's hand. "Let me make you a cup of tea." Taking Shirley's silence as agreement, Val switched on the kettle. She clattered about with milk and sugar, giving Shirley a chance to blow her nose and pull herself together. That also gave Val time to realise how hard it must have been for someone to take Angie's place. They'd judged Shirley only by the ways she'd differed from her predecessor and not given her much chance to earn their loyalty.

"It's so British, sorting things out with a cup of tea, isn't it?" Shirley said, when the drinks were ready.

Val smiled. "Angie used to say that. She chatted to us in our breaks and when we were rushed she'd make our tea."

"Good for Angie."

"Oops!" Val said. "I'm sorry, I meant to help by telling you how Angie did things, but I can see it comes across as criticism."

Shirley waved her apology away. "I can't say I've enjoyed the unfavourable comparisons, but it isn't the real problem. I'm coming under increasing pressure from the management. If targets aren't met, the whole department could be closed down and we'll all be out of a job."

"What!" No wonder Shirley had been so hard on everyone.

"I've said what they're expecting of you all isn't reasonable, but they said my predecessor managed it."

Val tried to make her voice gentle. "That's because we wanted to help her. We felt she was on our side, so we were on hers."

"I don't have that kind of loyalty, do I?"

"No, not exactly. You can't have a team behind you if you destroy the team feeling."

"You seemed to be getting on well just now." She gestured to the mutilated cartoon of herself and looked thoughtful. "It worked, didn't it? Your voodoo spell? You were laughing together and when you said you were to blame, I saw the others wanted to stick up for you – and would have done if you hadn't asked to discuss this privately. You've rebuilt the team."

"I suppose so."

Shirley tapped the sketch. "Could you draw another one of these for me, please?"

"I don't know what anyone in head office looks like," Val said.

Shirley laughed. "I might yet be tempted to stick pins into pictures of them, but this isn't for that. I'd like another one of me."

Val drew another quick cartoon, this time making it a little less unflattering.

"Thank you. I've seen people walking by; checking you're OK, I imagine?"

"They probably think I'm in a world of trouble. Am I?"

"No. No one is. Please go and tell them that and say I'll be out in a minute to talk to them."

Val was greeted by a barrage of questions. She had to repeat her, "No one is in trouble," message several times before it was believed, especially when she said Shirley was coming to talk to them. "I don't think she's as bad as she's seemed. She's had a lot to put up with, including getting grief from head office."

"Doesn't mean she has to take it out on us."

"No, but we've taken it out on her for not being Angie, haven't we?"

"That's because …" Tanya started to say.

Val interrupted with, "She's coming now."

Shirley held up the first mutilated sketch of herself. She gave everyone just long enough to see what it was and to imagine for a moment how Shirley must feel about their actions, before she screwed it up and threw it towards a bin.

It missed and Tanya picked it up and dropped it in.

"Thank you. Best place for it," Shirley said. Then she put the new one on the table. "Let's start afresh, shall we? Any suggestions?"

"I have." Julia grabbed a sheet of paper, drew a speech bubble and wrote 'Yes, Julia you may start twenty minutes later, so you can settle your autistic son into school and then work better without worrying quite so much.' She placed the words as though they were being spoken by the cartoon Shirley.

"I didn't know," Shirley said. "I should have done. Come and talk to me this afternoon and we'll try to work something out."

"Thanks."

"Anyone else?" Shirley asked. Quite bravely, Val thought.

Everyone took up sheets of paper or sticky notes and wrote or drew something. Most were complaints or requests for change, but someone cut out a smile and placed it over the severe expression Val had drawn. Someone else drew a funny hat.

"Thanks for your input everyone. Anyone got any glue?" Shirley stuck the hat and smile into place. "I'll keep this on my wall to remind myself not to take myself too seriously. And," she gestured to the pile of written comments, "I'll speak to you individually about all of these. Just to be clear, I'm not promising anything, but I will give you a chance to explain and if it seems reasonable to make a change then we will look for a way of doing that without any loss to the firm. OK?"

There were murmured agreements and everyone drifted back to their desks.

"Anything you'd like to add, Val?" Shirley asked.

"No, nothing."

In Val's hand was a sheet of paper on which she'd written 'Let's all go to Bangor.' She crumpled it up, just a Shirley, thankfully, had done with the first sketch of herself. Shirley wasn't Angie and it was unfair and unrealistic to expect her to behave in the same way. It was time to stop doing that and look for the good points in their new boss.

"That is, nothing except thank you for trying to save our jobs and that I look forward to a fresh start with our new boss."

Val remembered Shirley laughing at her offer to draw head office staff, and the way she'd stuck on her staff's improvements to the sketch of herself. Perhaps, once she'd settled in and was under less stress, Shirley would prove to be fun to work with.

9. Follow Your Nose

A sweet, almost spicy scent drew me down the garden. It wasn't unpleasant, far from it, but I couldn't identify which plant it might be coming from. That intrigued me. Until the last few months I'd been a very keen gardener and tried to fill my garden with year-round interest. Then I'd been made redundant. It was voluntary, so I should have been delighted to at last have time to get to grips with my slightly wayward plot, but it coincided with some bad news and a spell of dismal weather, so I spent less time, not more, outdoors.

I did make the effort to walk round occasionally and because of my years of watching gardening TV programmes, reading gardening books and pottering about, I thought I was familiar with most of my winter flowering plants, especially those with such nice perfume.

I decided it must be coming from the garden which backed onto mine, as it wasn't anything I'd planted. My eagerness to discover what it was got me tidying up my overgrown shrubs. The horticultural therapy helped lift my low mood.

After a couple of sessions I became aware my neighbour was doing his own pruning on the other side of the fence. We called out to each other whenever we were both working there at the same time.

"I hope you're another member of the escape committee?" he joked the first time.

I'm sure my response was equally daft, but it was good to

talk pleasantly to someone else.

It was weird chatting with someone I couldn't see, but I learned he'd moved in not long ago and was tackling the neglected garden.

"It should let more light into yours," he said.

Now and again he'd get me to look at a shrub so I could identify it for him and advise on whether he should cut it hard back then, or let it flower first. He indicated the one he meant by giving it a good shake. By the time we'd both worked our way through to the fence and could see each other through it, we felt like friends. There was something about him which reminded me of the one I'd recently lost.

I wasn't really surprised to hear Astrid had died. Saddened yes, but she'd been ill for some time so the bad news wasn't a real shock. I was surprised at how much I mourned her. We'd been friends since school. Us both having fairly unusual names was enough to form a kind of bond. Apparently I was supposed to be called Flora, after my gran, but Dad had been a bit emotional when he registered my birth and somehow added an L to the end.

Once Astrid and I missed out on a school trip. We didn't do it deliberately. In my case Mum had a puncture so I'd missed the coach. I can't remember what happened to stop Astrid going but as it was just the two of us from our form there, we were told we could either sit in on whichever lessons we liked, or spend the time in the library. We went to art first, then used our spending money to buy ingredients from the home economics teacher and made, iced and ate cakes all afternoon. The flavouring options were limited but we found ground cinnamon and vanilla extract. I chose cinnamon and Astrid used vanilla. We added them enthusiastically. When you're just thirteen it's definitely impossible to have too much of a good thing, so the fragrant spices went into the sponge, filling and the decorative icing.

After school we managed to get jobs in the same department store. Each morning we helped ourselves to a squirt of perfume from the cosmetics section. We did the same on our way out, being extra generous so it lasted into the evening. Astrid preferred the heavy, spicy scents. True to my name, I opted for floral. We sometimes joked that whenever we wanted to find each other, we just had to follow our nose.

When we were in our mid twenties we went on a training course in Manchester. Astrid met Sam and was soon spending more time up there with him than down South with me. We kept in touch however and I was invited to the wedding. Soon afterwards, Sam got an apparently unmissable job offer and they moved abroad. "We're going to follow our noses and look for adventure!" Astrid told me.

We still exchanged Christmas cards and the like. Not a regular correspondence at first, but I was always pleased to see Astrid's handwriting on an envelope. Astrid had always loved flowers I remembered and I'd become a keen gardener, so we often used pretty floral notepaper. Her letters were a joy to look at even before taking in the words. Reading them was almost like having her cheerful presence back in my life. I hope she felt that way about mine.

Sometimes we used postcards. I sent her one showing how a local landmark had been restored and another showing our pebbly beach was just the same as ever. She moved around a lot so sent me postcards of each new location.

Our relationship was like picture postcards. Always showing the best of everything. I don't mean we lied or bragged, just that we kept things light and positive. She told me about new friends she'd made, rather than those she'd had to leave. If I'd ended up almost doing a Mary Poppins impression with my umbrella I told her of the humour in the situation, not how I'd got soaked as a result of it becoming broken and useless.

She invited me to stay on several occasions, but I'm terrified of flying and kept making excuses. We met briefly a couple of times when she visited England, but it was just an hour, while her Sam did some shopping, between seeing her family and catching a train to see his.

Our letters became more frequent just when we both needed them most. She told me the chemo seemed to be working. I told her I was glad Phil and I had stopped rowing now he'd moved out. I looked for the positives to put in my letters to her and they helped me see them in my life. Tactfully, after I split up with mine, she didn't mention her husband in much detail, but I was sure he was a good man and they cared deeply for each other. After she told me she'd had to give up work because of her illness, I didn't say much about my own job, other than occasionally making fun of the dull bits and reminding her of the daft things we used to do to relieve the boredom when we'd worked together.

We made plans for getting together when she was strong enough to move back to England. She intended to return to her home town. Eating cake was firmly on the agenda, cinnamon and vanilla ones, naturally. Looking around my garden to admire my plants was also on the list. No date was set, but I told myself it really would happen and looked forward to it. I spoke in ever more glowing terms of my garden, home town and Britain in general in an effort to will her better and able to return.

I told her when my decree nisi came through, but I used

far more words describing the starlings in the birdbath. The day the divorce was made final I saw only the rain, but by the time I wrote to Astrid, I was already looking for rainbows.

Her letters too remained positive despite the fact that the pleasant things she'd seen were usually glimpsed from her window and the amusing people she'd met were hospital staff or fellow patients. Even as the letters got shorter and it was clear they'd been dictated, they were joky and lifted my spirits.

I didn't go to Astrid's funeral. Because of my reluctance to fly, she'd asked her husband not to notify me until it was too late to make the arrangements. He wrote and thanked me for my correspondence with Astrid, saying it had meant a great deal to her. Sam also said he intended to follow their plan and come back to England.

I should have replied immediately, but I hesitated so long that I assumed he'd have moved anyway by then. In truth, I didn't want to acknowledge that Astrid was gone. That loss coming at the same time as I gave up work and the weather turned wet and miserable and soon after my divorce made me give up on almost everything other than the mundane essentials of getting through life. Really I only walked around the garden because I couldn't stand staring at the TV any longer.

After smelling that mysterious plant, although I barely realised it, things began to improve. I only wore my older clothes for gardening, but made sure they were clean and my hair was brushed. By the time I came face to face with my new neighbour it was summer and I was wearing bright colours and a cheery expression. We didn't talk long, as his phone rang, but it was long enough for me to be glad we'd met at last and to think he seemed familiar somehow. I looked forward to our next conversation and to inviting him to look round my garden to get ideas for what might grow in his.

A few days later, as I walked past a tearooms, I was almost overpowered by the scent of cinnamon and vanilla. My mouth watered. It occurred to me that since hearing of Astrid's death I hadn't looked forward to anything. All the things I'd planned to do now I finally had time simply hadn't happened. One of them was treating myself to coffee and cake in town now and again. Maybe it would feel a little sad knowing that Astrid wouldn't ever be joining me, but from all I knew of her I thought it would be more disloyal to her memory to deny myself the pleasure, than to enjoy something we'd once briefly shared.

I stepped inside and immediately recognised the neighbour whose garden backed onto mine.

"Would you like to join me?" he said just as I started to ask if I might do that.

I placed my order and took a seat opposite him.

"I've just realised I don't know your name," he said. "I'm Sam." He offered his hand and I shook it.

Could the reason he seemed familiar be that I'd met him before, over thirty years previously? Sam isn't exactly an unusual name, but mine is and I looked for any trace of recognition as I gave it.

"My late wife had a friend called Floral," he said.

"You're Astrid's Sam?"

He was of course.

"You said you were thinking of coming back when you wrote to me," I said. "But I didn't realise it would be to this town."

"Neither did I. I'm from Manchester originally, but decided to revisit some of the places Astrid had talked about, or shown me on our trips home. As I walked through the town I got a really strong whiff of vanilla. It's a scent Astrid often wore when we first dated and I still associate it with her."

The waitress brought my coffee and carrot cake just then. Inhaling the fragrance of the cinnamon dusted over the top meant I could easily understand that. For a moment I could picture her aged twelve.

Sam continued, "This will probably sound weird, but just before she died, Astrid whispered 'follow your nose,' so I tried to trace the source of the scent."

"That doesn't sound weird to me," I assured him.

"No? Well, this might. It led me to an estate agent's. When I looked straight at a house for sale in Perfume Lane, it seemed as though she was trying to tell me something so I asked for the details."

"And moved into the house behind mine."

I didn't tell him then about the mysterious fragrant plant I'd been searching for when I first came across him at the bottom of the garden, or the vanilla and cinnamon which brought me there that day, but I will. I too think that Astrid was trying to tell me something, and that together Sam and I will find out exactly what that is.

10. Wishing Well

"Kelly! It's so good to see you!" Aurora hugged her best friend. "Oh, sorry, I've covered you in flour."

"Don't worry about that. Thanks to the terrible trio," Kelly gestured at the three angelic looking little girls, aged from three to six, "a dusting of flour is neither here nor there. Actually I'm pleased to see it. You sounded so frantically busy on the phone yesterday, I wasn't sure you'd even have time to stop for a cuppa, but if you're baking …"

"No, no. Come in all of you." Aurora plastered on a smile to hide the fact she'd been so frantically busy she'd completely forgotten Kelly had said she'd be popping in.

"Making cakes?" the middle child asked hopefully.

"No, sweetie. It's bread. I've got cookies though." Thankfully she'd bought a good selection of biscuits and soft drinks that morning. "They're in that bag over there. You three open the packets and put them in the cookie jar, OK?" To Kelly she said, "People are coming to view the house later and the estate agent suggested baking bread and arranging flowers to create the right atmosphere for a cottage."

"I've heard of things like that helping sales. Wouldn't brewing coffee have been easier?"

"The percolator's in storage!" Aurora declared.

"You said that with feeling."

"It's so frustrating, Kelly. Life's three times as difficult as it should be."

Her friend reached out and squeezed Aurora's shoulder. "What's happened? Are you and Dan OK?"

"Yeah, yeah we're fine. It's just all so complicated." Her whole life was.

The cottage had belonged to her grandparents. It was small and basic, with no room for what were now considered essentials such as a washing machine, dishwasher and tumble drier. There hadn't even been a proper bath, let alone a spare room for guests. An overnight visit meant washing in the sink and sleeping on an airbed in the living room. A longer stay involved a tin bath in front of the fire. Even so Aurora had loved staying there. Of course spending time with her granny was the biggest attraction, but she'd loved the little cottage too. That's probably why she'd eventually inherited it.

Aurora had been living there when she met Dan and had rented it out when they moved in to a characterless, although very practical, modern flat together. That flat was their first joint rung on the property ladder, Dan said. The first step to somewhere much better. Now, five years and almost as many moves later, they were buying a gorgeously converted factory workshop. Both the house they were living in and the cottage were to be sold to pay for it. They'd had a great offer on the house, provided they vacate immediately.

When Dan apologetically suggested coming back to the cottage, rather than risk losing the sale, she'd been rather pleased. She'd always liked it and thought it would be nice to spend a bit more time there before saying goodbye to it permanently. It hadn't been the homecoming she'd expected. Having Kelly close again was a real blessing, but otherwise it was stressful. The cottage was far smaller than their old place and they were going somewhere bigger still, hence a lot of stuff going into storage.

"It feels like camping," Aurora said. "And you know how I feel about that!"

"Don't I just."

As Aurora pummelled the risen dough, she said, "I suppose it's not that bad really. It's just with people coming to view all the time, we can't really relax and live here normally. Most things are great. I've got a great man, a job I love, and the next house will be fabulous. It's in very sought after location, lots of original features, good transport links …"

"Aunty Rora, why crying?" Kelly's youngest asked. All three girls tried to hug her.

"I'm not, sweetie. I'm just being silly." Aurora stopped tormenting the bread. The recipe said to 'knock it back', hers looked like she'd knocked it out. She put it in the oven; it would smell like bread, even if the result ended up the texture of cement.

"You're not at all happy, are you?" Kelly said.

"I am. Of course I am, it's just… I don't know, I just feel pulled in so many different directions."

That was true, but she was used to multi-tasking and it didn't usually bother her at all.

Kelly's girls chattered and wanted attention constantly. Kelly kept them occupied, made the drinks and listened to her friend, seeming totally calm and serene the whole time.

"You look after those three brilliantly, look after your house and lovely garden, volunteer at the shelter, are always there for family and friends. How do you do all that without thinking that whatever you're doing, you should be doing something else?"

"It's not so hard. You just have to accept you can't do everything and concentrate on what's really important."

"Everything is. I know I should take a break from getting ready for the viewing, to talk to you, but I daren't. This place needs to sell quickly or we'll need a bridging loan, or lose the workshop. We've both had to take time off work so have loads to catch up on. When we've not been cleaning, decorating, packing and driving for hours between here and work, we're in our offices or on the laptops, so I barely see Dan. Mum can't understand why, now I'm just back down the road, we can't waste a whole Sunday having lunch with her, and I can't be taking her here there and everywhere."

Kelly hugged her, then found a tissue so she could blow her nose. Once Aurora was a bit calmer, her friend asked, "Did you say flower arranging was on your list for today?"

"Ideally, but please don't tell me that will help me relax. I forgot to buy any and …"

Kelly held up a hand to silence her. "Girls, would you like to help Aunty Aurora and pick her some flowers?"

They agreed enthusiastically and went out with instructions not to step off the tiny, overgrown lawn. Cutting that would have made more sense than kneading bread, but lately Aurora seemed to have lost the ability to focus on what was important. Had she really just described visiting her much loved Mum as a waste of time and paid more attention to bread nobody would eat than her best friend and those lovely kids?

Once the girls were outside, Kelly said, "Look, this will sound mad, but you remember when I thought I'd never get pregnant?"

Of course Aurora did. Her friend had been distraught.

"I got help... You have to promise not to tell anyone unless they're in real need."

"OK." Who would she tell anyway? She hardly had time for a conversation.

"I visited a holy well," Kelly startled her by saying. "A lady at work said how much it helped her. It really did, and it helped me, and I know of a few others, but it doesn't have unlimited power. If people go there asking for trivial things then it won't be there for those who really need it."

"Oh, Kelly! I know you're just trying to help, but I haven't got time to mess about with that sort of thing!"

"You don't have time for me now either, do you?" She sounded really hurt.

What could Aurora say? She'd been trying to sneak a look at her work emails whilst Kelly was talking. If she kept on like this, she was likely to upset everyone close to her.

"It'll be even worse when you move away again," Kelly pointed out. "Do me, and yourself, a favour and agree to take a couple of hours off this weekend and spend it with me."

"Visiting a holy well?"

"Yep. First though, I'll clean up in here, get the flowers sorted and take the bread out when it's done. You go do whatever else you need to."

"Really?"

"Of course. I came to help."

By the time Aurora returned from changing out of her flour covered clothes and blasting through the most urgent work tasks, the cottage smelled homely. It wasn't just the bread; Kelly had mown the lawn. The children's unsophisticated flower arrangements in jugs and glasses looked absolutely right. The estate agent would be delighted and Aurora felt almost in control of her life again. She knew it was temporary, but the relief was enormous.

"Thank you so much!"

"I'll pick you up Saturday at ten," Kelly said just before she drove away.

On the way to the well, the girls chattered excitedly about going to the fairy grotto.

Kelly explained, "I, and others who've benefitted, visit with positive thoughts and leave tokens of gratitude. Somehow it seems right, as though that might replenish its power or something. As a result it looks… Oh, you'll see." She parked the car and they all set off through the woods.

Aurora gasped when she reached the small clearing, studded with colourful wild flowers. Hundreds of ribbons were tied onto nearby trees. The well itself was just a gently bubbling pool surrounded by a low stone wall, covered in moss. It was unpretentious and full of charm. The girls were right, it did look as though fairies had been there. There was something almost spiritual about it.

Aurora started to think she'd been right to come. Maybe it was all the tokens of gratitude or perhaps the look on Kelly's face as she'd tied up tiny fragments of ribbon taken from those she used for the girls' hair. More likely it was taking a break from all the frantic activity so she had the chance to catch her breath. Lovely as the place was, Aurora still doubted it had magical powers.

"We'll go for a walk now and leave you in peace to think," Kelly said. "The well will help, I promise – but only once for a single issue. You can't just say 'fix my life'. You need to be very specific about what you want. Visualise it being true and then dip your hand into the water."

Aurora was surprised at Kelly leaving, as she'd thought the real point was for them to have time together. They were almost inseparable at one point, spending all their free time together, except the week each summer when Kelly went to guide camp. This was for real then? Kelly believed the well had helped her and would do the same for Aurora. As she was there, and unable to get on with anything else on her to-do list, she may as well try.

Aurora knew what her problem was; she had far too much to do, was stressed out and couldn't cope. No one specific wish could fix that, so what was she going to ask for? She didn't want to be thinner or prettier or famous – the kind of things she'd have asked for as a teenager. Dan had fallen in love with her just as she was. She'd kept herself looking presentable for work, but otherwise not really given a great deal of thought to her appearance, so clearly that wasn't a priority. Unlike her friend, she'd never desperately wanted children. Maybe it would happen, she hoped it would, but she and Dan hadn't discussed the matter. Lately they hadn't talked about anything important, just their next move onwards and upwards.

She didn't need a better job, as with the move she'd get one. Her company had agreed not only that she transfer, but had offered the promotion. She hadn't told Dan, but they'd offered it before and she'd turned it down because she'd been so happy where she was. It was challenging and fulfilling, she worked with a great team and at the time they hadn't needed the extra money. With the move she'd have to change jobs anyway, get to deal with new challenges, build a relationship with the new team, so moving up a level made sense. Although not something she'd sought, the new job wasn't what had her so… Upset? Unsettled?

Was it Dan then? She was aware she'd held back thinking of him, when really he should have come first. Did she suspect something was wrong? No; even now she allowed herself to think about it, no problems leapt to mind. They didn't row, he wasn't unkind to her in any way, she was certain he wasn't being unfaithful. When would he have the time for an affair? Or to argue, come to that. They didn't talk much, apart from making plans for a better future.

Was it her? Did she not love Dan? She thought she did, but lately it felt like she hardly knew him, or even herself. Asking the well to fix her relationship was no good. She couldn't be at all specific there as she didn't know if there was a problem to solve, or if she wanted it fixed even if there was.

The new house then? Was that the problem? No, that was silly. The place was gorgeous and there were so many advantages. It was huge, and light and airy. There was a fabulous kitchen, a bathroom so luxurious that even brushing her teeth would feel like a spa break. The views of the city and the river were spectacular. So close to just about everything, including a train station so she could easily go back home and visit…

That was it. A home was what she wanted, not a base for the next desperate push onwards and upwards. Somewhere she'd feel settled and relaxed. The new place wouldn't be that. Dan had spoken of it as an investment and how one day she'd once again be able to have a garden. That would mean another move. More stress, more hours working to pay for it.

"I want a home," Aurora said, and dipped her hand into

the water. She'd expected it to be cold, but it wasn't exactly… Nor was it warm. It felt as though she'd made a connection. Whatever magic was in the well, she'd set it to work.

What had she done? Dan was working as hard as Aurora to make the purchase of the converted workshop go through. How would he react if it didn't happen? She could lose him. She'd certainly lose her new job. Everything would change – or rather nothing would. She'd be taking a step or more back to when she and Dan had first met…

Or would she? Dipping her hand in water didn't prove anything. Now she thought about it, it hadn't done anything for Kelly either. She wasn't a mother but a stepmother. Her adoration for the girls was so completely returned that it was easy to forget that.

Kelly came back. She waited on the edge of the clearing and held out her hands as though asking a question.

Aurora went over to her and the girls, who each held bunches of cow parsley and buttercups.

"Go and put the flowers on the wall, but don't go inside," she told them. When they ran off, she asked if Aurora had made her wish.

"Yes, but then I realised it didn't matter. This doesn't work, does it? You asked to be pregnant and …"

"No, I didn't. I meant to be specific and ask for a baby of my own, but somehow I said I wanted a family; children to love and who'll love me, and I have that."

"Yes, you do," Aurora agreed.

"Simon had asked me to marry him before I came here, but I'd worried I was interested in him for the wrong reasons. Coming here showed me that yes, I wanted the girls as much as the man, but that was OK because they were a complete package. A family. My family."

"So the well didn't bring you what you wanted, so much as show you what that was?"

"Exactly. What did you ask for? Or would you rather not say?"

"I asked for a home. Oh! I never said which home. I need to talk to Dan, don't I? Make sure we're not both just caught up in this madness of working towards something we're not sure we really want."

A year later, Aurora and Dan returned, carrying flowers. When they reached the edge of the clearing, he gestured for her to go ahead. She arranged moon daisies, pink campion and bluebells on the wall surrounding the well, then knelt and dipped her hand into the crystal clear water and thought positive, grateful thoughts.

After visiting the well with Kelly, she'd gone back to the cottage and told Dan they must talk. "No phones or laptops, just us. And no saying what we think the other wants to hear."

"What's this about?" he'd asked, unsurprisingly looking a little concerned.

"The future. Our future… Or futures. I want to know what you really want, not what you think you should be working for, or what's expected, but what you truly want." She explained about her visit to the well, and how it had made her realise she'd lost sight of that herself, and felt maybe he had too. "We can't work towards what we want unless we know what that is."

The discussion continued over the next few days. His

answers had nothing to do with investment potential, bridging loans, or quick sales. They did involve yet more changes and disruption to their lives, but this time she felt it would be worth the inconvenience and extra work.

As she'd been remembering, Dan had approached the well and stood by her side. She reached for his hand to help herself up. It felt damp, just as if he'd dipped it into the water.

"Did you want to be alone for a moment and make a wish?" she asked him.

"No, I was just saying thank you because I already have everything I want." He turned her hand so the diamond in her ring sparkled like the water in the well. "You, soon to be my wife, and now the extension to the cottage is almost complete, a home where we can stay, be happy, and grow old together."

11. Romance Is Dead

Hearing an agonised cry, Lisa raced upstairs. With heart hammering in her chest she watched her deathly pale daughter lurch across the bedroom.

"What's happening?"

"I'm practising my zombie look." Her tone said 'duh' even though Monique bit back the word.

"It's horrible."

"Great! Thanks, Mum."

Lisa went back downstairs. "I despair of that girl, I really do."

"Oh?" Adam didn't even look up from his paper.

"She used to be such a sweet little thing, interested in clothes, make-up and romance."

"Wears plenty of make-up if you ask me."

"I preferred the sort that gives her a pink complexion, not greyey-green. And call me old-fashioned but I like lipstick to stay on the lips, not drip down as though she's been drinking blood. I want my romantic little girl back."

"Romance is dead," Adam said.

"Undead more like. She's pretending to be a zombie."

"Exactly." He said that as though there was nothing to worry about.

Of course there really wasn't anything to worry about. At sixteen Monique had plenty of time to find love. Not that having a man in her life was everything these days. Nor had it been when Lisa was a teenager. Plenty of girls then had chosen careers over family, had alternative relationships, or just preferred the single life. If that's what Monique wanted she'd support her, of course she would.

Lisa gave herself a shake. Monique was happy, healthy and doing well at school. It wasn't Monique she was worried about, but herself. Lisa had loved it when her daughter borrowed her clothes and asked for lessons applying make-up. Clothes shopping with her was so much fun and her heart melted when Monique confided over her first crush. Lisa had expected that to continue. She'd imagined herself giving relationship advice, giggling over outrageous fashions and eventually planning a wedding.

Then Monique met the mysterious Hilary. 'Hilary says' and 'Hilary thinks' became the opening remarks to almost all Monique's conversation. Lisa couldn't quite put her finger on it, but there was something about Hilary which made her uneasy. Maybe it was just that she'd never met the girl.

"Why don't you invite Hilary for tea after school?" she'd suggested.

"Oh, Muuuuuum." If Lisa had suggested Monique walk to school holding her mother's hand, she'd probably have got a more positive response.

All Lisa could gather was Hilary was eighteen and studying drama. Hilary didn't appear to share any of Monique's interests, other than the current obsession with zombies. Lisa had tried coaxing out information, but every query resulted in another, "Oh, Muuuum," and sometimes an eye roll too.

Monique had stopped confiding in her. Instead it was her dad she talked to. Which was good of course. Lisa was in no way jealous of her husband's new closeness to their daughter.

She took a cup of tea in to Adam. "Do you think this Hilary is a good influence on Monique?" she asked. "She's changed so much."

"Aaaw, leave her alone," Adam said. "You were just the same at that age. I remember you dyeing your lovely hair jet black and swapping your cute skirts for horrible white trousers. Nearly put me off."

Lisa laughed. "I only did it because you were so into Queen."

"Great sound, but I didn't want to date Freddie Mercury."

"I suppose not. So, what you're saying is, she's just going through a phase and it'll be OK?"

"It might well be a phase and I'm certain it'll be OK, but that isn't what I said."

"Muuuum!" came a cry. Not the 'Mum you're soooo dim' version, but the 'Mum, I need a favour right now' version.

Lisa raced upstairs.

Monique's living-dead make up was still in place, but she was changing her clothes. "Hilary called. We were going to film in the sports hall, but as it's raining they're doing tennis inside, so I was wondering …"

"You'd like Hilary to come here?"

"Yeah, but you won't be weird, will you?"

By then Monique had changed from ripped baggy shirt and jeans, to skimpy top and short shorts. She made an artful tear in the top, exposing a portion of toned midriff and applied more green make-up over her healthy looking tan.

"I'll try not to be," Lisa said.

Monique got busy with her mobile, then said, "So, how do I look?"

"Undead?"

"In a good way?"

"It's not what I'd call attractive, but I suppose that's not the look you're going for."

"But if it was?"

"Well, I'd do something different with your hair and tone down the green and purple on your face."

"Help me?"

"Of course." Making her daughter look beautifully undead rather than almost putrid wasn't quite the mother and daughter activity she longed for, but better than nothing. She set to work.

Monique's phone buzzed. "That's Hilary now, I'll go and let him in."

"Him?"

"Er, yeah? He's doing a short film called *Romance Is Dead* and I'm playing his zombie girlfriend."

"Oh!"

"You didn't think I'd be putting myself through all this unless it was to get a hot guy, did you?" Monique winked.

Downstairs again, Lisa greeted Hilary. He seemed very charming for a man who looked like he didn't have a pulse. She did her best not to be weird as she offered coffee and a snack.

"Still despairing?" Adam asked when they went to film a scene in the garage.

"Yes! She's so like I was at that age, I dread to think what they'll be getting up to out there!"

12. He Always Bought Me Roses

My instincts scream that someone has been in the house since I left for work this morning. There's no sign anything is wrong, no reason for me to get worked up. Except, just like the rest of me, my imagination knows what day it is. Pity it's forgotten I've never been scared of Friday the thirteenth and I don't care about the other significance of today's date.

I check the door. No damage and it's still locked. I let myself in. The hallway is as warm and welcoming as always. My shivering is simply a reaction to the gloomy afternoon. The clocks going back unsettles everyone.

My heart beats faster when I see the kettle is askew and there's a dirty mug in the sink. Usually I'm not so lazy. It's a lesson I've learned well; learned the hard way. Perhaps I left them like that as an act of defiance? There's a first time for everything. You'd think I'd remember, but I wasn't at my best this morning. Couldn't sleep last night. Nervous anticipation.

I wash the mug, dry it thoroughly and put it away, straighten the kettle. That's better. No one need know I was slovenly this morning. If I was. Of course it was me who left it out. I live alone now. Alone in this empty house.

The faint citrus tang in the air might be flooding my memory with thoughts of damp skin and a freshly shaved face, but it's the washing-up liquid I can smell. Probably. Fear has always made my senses more acute. The drizzle falling on the roof sounds like the shower running. The saliva in my mouth tastes like blood from a split lip.

I run into the lounge. Stumble against the coffee table. Put out my hands to save myself and dislodge the sofa cushions. That's why they're out of line. I did it myself just now. No one has been here. No one but clumsy me. How many times must I be told to be more careful? It's OK, I haven't done anything which could get me hurt. I'm just a bit jumpy, that's all.

Maybe, knowing what I'm like, I should have had someone with me or gone to Mum's today. Trouble is I know what she's like too. I don't need yet another lecture on the evils of my ex-husband – as though I might have already forgotten the bruises and broken bones. Not that she knows about those. She guessed, but doesn't truly know what it was like between us. The bad and the good. Just like she doesn't know I haven't actually done the paperwork yet. I couldn't face the publicity of divorcing him during the court case. And then his sentence was so short it seemed better to wait until afterwards.

I hardly know I'm looking for anything until I see it. On my bedside table, in a tiny crystal vase, is a white rose. Just the one perfect bloom. The way my heart beats is a sign of fear. I don't know who, but someone has broken into my home. It could have been anyone. Some else's lover who got the wrong address, a stalker, some random axe murderer. But it's not. I know it's not.

For one thing it wasn't an axe. For another he wasn't convicted of murder. I didn't testify. The law couldn't make me. Nothing could have made me, so all they got him for was stealing from the corpse. I didn't testify to that either, but the victim's blood was on his clothes and his credit cards in my husband's pocket.

Cliff was released today. It's only halfway through his sentence, but his behaviour has been good. That must mean something, surely? He was so sweet when we first met. So gentle. He used to buy me roses every week.

The shower stops running.

He's home.

I wait. It's what I've been doing since they took him away.

He walks out of the bathroom wearing just a towel. "Come here, babe."

My dreams and my nightmares come true as I step into his arms and eagerly lift my face for his kiss.

13. Night Watchman

My mate Jim told me about a job vacancy in the self storage unit. "He always seems to need new people and the pay is good."

"Is there much paperwork involved?" I asked. A mix-up over figures at my last place was why I needed a job.

"Wouldn't have thought so. They want a night watchman. You fancy it, Mark?"

"Of course." I saw his frown. "I've done a bit of security work before," I told him.

"It's not that… I've heard some strange rumours."

"Haven't I told you not to listen to gossip?" I teased.

Jim shrugged and tapped the number into his mobile phone for me. Five minutes later I'd arranged an interview.

To start with the boss seemed worried the unsocial hours would be a problem. When I explained I live alone and don't have any commitments which make night work difficult he became friendlier.

"I don't read or write very well," I admitted.

"Not a problem," the boss said. "Tell you what, I'll pay you cash in hand and you won't have any official paperwork to deal with."

"Does that mean I've got the job?"

"Yes, Mike. But your employment is subject to you having no police record," he warned me. "I'll check up on that."

"No problem," I assured him.

"I'll see you here at ten tonight then," he said as he shook my hand.

"Right. Will my predecessor give me a handover and explain my duties?" That's what's happened most other places where I've worked.

"He's… unavailable. I'll do that myself."

After I'd thanked Jim for helping me get the job, I mentioned that. "Something about the way he said it seemed odd."

"I think I know why. Apparently some gang had been hiding stolen loot there. The police did a midnight raid and there were rumours the security guard was in on it and got sacked, or that it spooked him and he quit."

The boss was waiting when I arrived and went through my duties in more detail.

He showed me the incident log. "If you write your full name now, just your initials and the date when you go on and off duty will be fine from then on. If you need to record anything else, just a few words are all you need and you can give me the details in person."

He made tea as I laboriously completed the entry, which was tactful. More so than Jim really; he does any writing for me.

"We take the security of our customer's belongings very seriously," the boss said as we drank our brew. "Their confidentiality is important too. We take care to ensure that only one client goes into an area at once and that they're undisturbed by staff."

"Right. Sure." That part didn't concern me. As a night

watchman I'd never deal with anyone who rented storage space. Hopefully I wouldn't ever deal with anyone who hoped to gain illegal access to the contents either.

As I was shown round, that possibility seemed reassuringly unlikely. The fence and gate were formidable. The doors and locks on all the units looked impressive. There was floodlighting, CCTV, an alarm system, and me on patrol five nights a week. The dates were picked randomly so anyone checking wouldn't know when there was someone on duty.

"On no account are you to enter any storage rooms yourself," my boss insisted.

"Got it." Theoretically I could. There's a pass key in case a client loses their own, but they have to go through so much hassle to prove who they are that it's rarely called into use.

"If there is any kind of... situation, which you feel requires entry to any storage room, you're to call me and I will attend to it. Are we clear about that?"

I assured him we were.

The job was easy. All I had to do was keep a watch on the CCTV monitors and walk round now and again. I never needed to write anything, other than the times I arrived and left, in the log. Just as well really, with my dyslexia.

"How's the job going?" Jim asked me when I happened to bump into him a few days later.

"It's fine."

"You never get scared there at night?" It was an odd question for him to ask.

"Nope." Truth is I'd never had cause to be. Don't suppose I'd be very brave if someone waved a gun in my face and demanded access, but it wasn't going to happen.

"Isn't it creepy in the dark?" he asked another time.

"The place is lit up like a Christmas tree and I carry a torch."

Things do look different in artificial light; they appear unreal, but not necessarily more creepy because of that. Actually my biggest problem was boredom. Reading is so much effort that it's no pleasure and if I'd listened to music I couldn't have listened out for trouble so wouldn't be doing my job properly.

Anyone with too much imagination would have had plenty of opportunity to scare themselves stupid wondering if the creakings were footsteps, or if the wind was calling to them. Not me. OK, a couple of times I did hear something which sounded like a voice, but how could it have been?

Every night I carried out my patrols, varying it a bit by going clockwise if the hour was an even one and clockwise at eleven, one, three and five. In between I watched the CCTV monitors. There was often a flash of lights as a car passed. A few times I saw a fox go by just outside the fence. Litter got blown about sometimes and created hugely distorted shadows, which seemed to leap up against storerooms, or run down passageways. I could play back the recordings if I wasn't sure. I chided myself the times I did that because my imagination had run away with me.

Mostly there wasn't even the excitement of an unusual shadow. To relieve the boredom I flicked through the incident log. Letters and numbers don't stay still on the page for me, so it took me a while to learn Jim had been half right about the police business. It did happen, but was over a year ago and wasn't the reason for the night watchman involved leaving this job, as his initials continued for another fortnight. Then one day he signed in but not out.

Over the next few nights I looked through the log more thoroughly. In the past three years there had been six different night security staff. One woman and five men. I knew because, just like me, when they'd started the first night they'd written in their full names. Thankfully, also like me, they used short words, and very few of them, in any reports. One had been on duty during a brief power cut. He'd recorded that and the fact that all systems were soon fully operational again. Another mentioned a sign coming loose during a storm. That was it. So why had they all left so soon? And why had they all signed in for their last shift, but not out again?

Between patrols, I painstakingly checked and rechecked all the entries. There didn't seem to be anything the previous watchmen all had in common. They'd worked for different periods of time. They hadn't all left on the same date or day of the week, though I wouldn't have been able to explain it if they had.

I borrowed a diary from Jim, thinking that might help. Silly really. If it had been hallowe'en or something like that then they'd each have left a year apart. And of course hallowe'en isn't any reason for security staff to clock off unexpectedly. Or rather not clock off.

It had been full moon the night the only female security guard had last signed in. Hmm, full moon fell on different dates, didn't it? It was about a month ago I'd thought I'd heard a voice and I had a feeling it was a full moon then… I couldn't remember the exact date. Who would? The full moon before that was just before I started. The night my predecessor left.

Coincidence obviously. I told myself that for days. Right until the next full moon, which was when I heard the voice.

No, I hadn't gone mad. This was an actual voice, not some ghostly moaning. A real voice begging for food. Ghosts don't eat. I followed the sound and located the storage room.

"Anyone in there?" I yelled.

"Yes! Please help me. I'm so hungry, so weak."

"What's happened? How did you get stuck in there?" Surely the rooms could be opened from the inside?

"I don't remember. There was food at first, but it's gone now."

They'd been kidnapped? It sounded far-fetched, but I couldn't think of anything more plausible.

"Don't worry, I'll get you out of there."

I ran down to get the pass key. It was in one of those things where you have to smash the glass. There was also a sign. In my panic I might not have been able to read it, but I already knew it was a warning to call the boss if the key were needed.

Would he want me to call at three in the morning? He had said to call no matter what the situation, and put his number on speed dial in the office phone so it was easy for me to do that. Besides, he'd have to know about the trapped man at some point. I rang.

"I'm coming. Do not open that door. Wait until I get there."

I agreed, but went to reassure the trapped man that help was on the way.

"Thank you, but hurry please. I feel so faint."

Were the containers airtight? Was he slowly suffocating?

"How long have you been in there?" I asked.

No reply.

I ran back to the office, smashed the glass and extracted the key to save time for when the boss arrived. Next I went down and opened the gates so he could drive right in, and left the door to the unit standing open.

Then I went back. "Help will be here really soon," I assured the occupant.

Still no answer. He wouldn't have died from hunger surely, not if he was strong enough to shout before? But he could have passed out if there wasn't enough oxygen. Or maybe he'd been injured and lost a lot of blood. I opened the door just a tiny bit and shone my torch inside.

It was like the set of a horror movie. The smell was horrible. Of course it was; the poor man had been shut in there for days. He was lying in a corner. He looked barely alive. Barely human. Like a shell of a man. I put my hand up to his mouth to see if I could feel breathing. Nothing. I'd cut my hand fetching the key and a drop of blood dripped onto his lips, but that brought no reaction.

Then the voice again asked for food. It came from the body in front of me, but the mouth hadn't moved. Jumping back in fear and confusion, I knocked it. The body rocked gently. Not a body, but a plastic mould!

Laughing at my own stupidity, I flipped it over and saw the compartment which held the batteries… was empty.

The thing sat up and licked the drop of blood from its lip. "Delicious." It gave a horrible smile. "But I need much more."

"I warned you!" a voice hissed from behind me. The boss. "I said not to go in there." He lurched towards me.

A strong hand grabbed my arm. I thought it was the thing, drawing his supper closer, and fainted.

When I came to, I was in the corridor with Jim bending over me. "Thought you didn't get scared?" he said.

I'd been beyond scared, still was. "Where's the boss?"

Jim pointed to the storage room. "I remembered you said it was really important that staff don't go in and that clients aren't disturbed in their own storage rooms. This one is in his name, so I shoved him aside and dragged you out."

You might be wondering how a guy with such bad dyslexia has managed to write this story. That's easy; I haven't. Jim's done it for me. As a journalist he's much better at that sort of thing than me. And as a journalist he'd taken an interest in the rumours about staff from the storage facility going missing and persuaded his mate, me, to go undercover for him. To shine a light onto the situation, you might say. I didn't mind helping, but I wish that now it's all over I could switch off that light, close my eyes and see nothing but the darkness.

14. Little Savage

She stared, fascinated as his sharp little teeth ripped at the lump of fresh, red, flesh. The sight appalled her, yet she could not look away. Sara knew she dare not take her eyes off him, not even for a moment.

Holding the skin firmly, he feasted on the juicy interior. Greedily he bit off chunks; eating noisily and chuckling with pleasure. He wiped his hand across his face, dispersing the crimson liquid that ran freely from his mouth.

What a savage little monster, thought Sara as she watched her two-year-old son eat his first slice of watermelon.

15. Conservatory Of The Imagination

"I picked up details of a house today," Fergal said. "Want to look?"

Donna knew she should be interested. They'd always planned to move from the city flat to somewhere in the countryside with a big garden, as soon as they could afford it. The new house would have room for children to play and their family to grow.

They didn't need that now, but Donna couldn't stay where she was, in rooms filled with unhappy memories. Neither could she summon the energy and enthusiasm to do anything about it.

Aware Fergal was waiting for a response, she shrugged. "Maybe."

Disappointment showed in Fergal's face. Just a flicker, swiftly hidden. It wasn't for himself, Donna knew. She'd told him she was getting better and he'd tried to believe her. She thought she really was at times.

The joy when she thought she was finally pregnant had been short lived. Donna discovered the longed for baby was a tumour. She'd had radical treatment and recovered physically. Emotionally though…

Donna was left with the money to buy the house she wanted, but nothing that would make it a home.

Fergal brought mugs of tea and sat beside her.

"Sorry," she said as she curled her hands around hot china.

"For what?" Fergal asked.

"Feeling sorry for myself again."

Although it often felt that way, it wasn't true she had nothing good in her life. She had Fergal's unwavering love. He too had wanted the child which never was, but learning it never would be hadn't changed how he felt about her. They had other family too; his parents and brother, Donna's sister, brother-in-law and their children. She'd have hope to, if she could make herself look forward. They'd talked about the possibility of adopting, when she felt ready. If she ever felt ready.

Fergal didn't speak, just squeezed her shoulder. Another thing to be grateful for, he never pretended everything was OK.

Donna pulled herself together and asked about his day.

He explained about work, then visiting the estate agency and picking up the paperwork. "I'm sure you'd like it. It's got a conservatory."

She'd always liked conservatories. Her grandparents had a tiny one. Too hot in summer, too cold in winter but that's where the toys were and where Donna and her sister could make as much mess and noise as they liked. She'd had her first kiss in a conservatory. It was Fergal who'd done the deed. She'd kissed other boys during the next few years, but eventually married her first love. Their wedding reception had been in a huge conservatory attached to a grand hotel.

After learning she wasn't pregnant and never would be, she'd built a conservatory in her imagination and often retreated there. It was a mix of gothic architecture and art deco tiles. Hot and humid. There was lots of intricate ironwork, not so much glass. A place designed for hiding in, not looking out of. Donna had mentally filled it with orchids, their fat buds swelling. Bright colours might burst forth at any moment, but she hadn't yet imagined the blooms. She felt safe there. Comforted to some extent, but knew it wasn't a real place and didn't want it to be.

Fergal squeezed her shoulder again and Donna gulped down almost cold tea. "Where's this leaflet then?" she asked in what she hoped was a cheerful voice.

She concentrated hard on reading the words and looking at the photos, taking in the details of the house and not being distracted by her grief. The brochure described a house just like the one they'd always wanted. Big rooms and plenty of them. A decent sized garden and open countryside beyond.

"It seems nice, but they always do with these things." Donna tried to sound realistic, rather than unwilling to believe she might like it.

"True. You definitely have to see places for yourself."

"Yes," Donna said.

"Yes you agree, or yes …?"

"Yes, I'll come and see it."

Fergal looked so pleased. "We won't let them push us into a decision," he told her. The reassurance wasn't just about pressure from the estate agent.

The house seemed lovely from the outside and the location was good. Donna felt almost optimistic. Inside they discovered the kitchen had been partially ripped out, the bathrooms were non-operational and the conservatory leaked.

The estate agent talked about potential. No working plumbing didn't sound like a great opportunity to Donna, but she could see potential in the conservatory. Unlike the one she'd built in her mind, this had big sheets of glass and an airy feel. If the glass was cleaned, light would flood in. Even through the grime she saw that the conservatory pushed right into the garden, providing views in three directions. The garden was enclosed by a low hedge. Beyond that was farmland, woods and a river. The scene would change through the seasons and give pleasure every month of the year.

Donna could imagine sitting there. Not hiding; looking out onto the world beyond. She could imagine children playing in the garden. Her nieces and nephews could visit. It would be great for those city kids to have the space and freedom to run around. Donna returned to the conservatory of her imagination as she and her husband were dragged around the rest of the property. She mentally enlarged the glass panels, letting in more light, allowing glimpses of the world beyond.

As they drove home, Fergal said, "I didn't realise how much work was needed. Sorry."

"It's not your fault. I read the same literature and didn't understand about the plumbing and things either."

"I don't think it's for us?" Fergal said.

"No. But there will be a right place. We'll keep looking."

"Really? You want to?"

"Yes. Definitely."

And later they would make enquiries about adoption. She wasn't ready yet, but one day she would be. One day she and Fergal would have a proper home, full of love, where they would create happy memories.

16. Past, Present And Future

It's three years since I first saw the haunted bauble. Of course back then I didn't believe it was haunted with the spirit of Christmas, mostly because I didn't believe in such a thing.

Nothing had gone right in my life for months. My unreliable boyfriend left me. My job was tedious. I suffered from vertigo, which made getting out of bed in the morning a worse than usual ordeal. The weather was as cold and grey as my mood. Was it surprising I'd turned into a biscuit-addicted semi-recluse?

Why socialise if I'd be a figure of gloom at every gathering? I couldn't drink with my medication. Couldn't eat because my clothes were already too tight. I couldn't afford more; my ex left me a debt as crippling as my broken heart.

Everyone said, "Stop feeling sorry for yourself. You'll feel better if you get into the Christmas spirit."

I didn't want to do anything anyone told me, or believe anything anyone said. Even so, I dragged myself round the shops looking for gifts and something to wear at my parents' home on Christmas Day.

I was in full Bah Humbug mode when I reached a shop called 'Christmas Marvels'. I went in, expecting to feel condescending towards people wasting their money on junk, but it wasn't like that. Although I'd not seen the shop before it wasn't one of those tacky looking efforts which appear in empty premises just for Christmas. This had an old-fashioned charm and gave the impression it had been there forever.

On offer were shiny little antiques, heirloom decorations and unusual gifts. I'd barely glanced round when I saw it: the bauble. Although pretty, it would have been far more my sort of thing if it had been a vase or a non Christmassy ornament. I didn't bother with decorations much at the best of times and certainly didn't intend to that year.

"You don't want that," the shopkeeper said.

I looked more closely. It was created from the most delicate clear glass, etched with tiny images of holly, ivy and mistletoe. It looked like ice and snow. Like frozen nature waiting for spring warmth. I wanted it so much.

"It's real crystal and the fitting is silver. It's very old, very expensive." She didn't actually sneer at me, but I heard one in her voice.

Mum had asked more than once what I'd like for Christmas. Other than my snapping 'for it to be over' she'd not got an answer.

"How much is it?" I asked.

"It's not for sale."

That convinced me I had to have it. "So why is it in the shop?"

"Didn't want it at home. It's haunted."

"I don't believe in ghosts."

"Not by a ghost, by a spirit of Christmas." That line wasn't convincing when Charles Dickens came up with the idea, but I kept the thought to myself and simply said, "Really?" with no attempt to hide my doubt.

"Buy this and everything will go wrong. You'll never find true love and this will be your worst ever Christmas."

Funnily enough I was willing to risk that. She was a brilliant saleswoman. If she'd told me it would make me happy I'd have lost interest immediately.

"It must stay in the family."

There was a tag I hadn't noticed before, marked £45.

"Then it shouldn't be in a shop with a price label on it." Hah! She didn't have an answer to that.

It seemed a ridiculous price for a Christmas bauble, even if it was really crystal, but Mum usually spent about that much on me and I didn't think she'd see it as a waste if she thought I really wanted the thing – which I did. A quick call confirmed she'd be pleased to buy me something pretty and Christmasy.

"Get it now and I'll give you the money when I see you."

"OK, I'll have it," I said to the saleswoman.

"If you must!"

Once I'd paid she was all smiles. Maybe she'd just thought I was a time waster?

"Is there anything else I can get you?" she asked.

I bought a jewellery box I was sure Mum would love, a smart pen for Dad and pretty brooches for my friends. Half an hour later I was home with a mug of tea and my shopping finished. The relief prompted me to arrange my cards round the room and suspend my new bauble in the window where it caught the light, showering the walls in tiny rainbows.

On Christmas morning, I sat on the edge of the bed until my vertigo subsided. Luckily it only bothered me first thing. I looked out; no snow. Good, Dad would have no trouble driving over to collect me. I had biscuits for breakfast, followed by a tangerine to make it a healthier meal. It was rather nice not having a hangover from the previous night's party and to have spent the evening giggling with friends instead of arguing with my ex or seeing him chatting up another girl. If we'd still been together the giggling might have happened, the hangover and row were an almost certainty.

Christmas Day wasn't wildly exciting. Neither was it horribly disappointing. It was quiet, cosy, pleasant. About three hundred times better than I'd expected.

Back at work on the 27th my colleagues must have been surprised at the change in my attitude. Tell the truth, so was I. If the 'Christmas Marvels' shopkeeper had told me everything would go right once I owned the bauble I'd probably have looked at everything in an unfavourable light, but that hadn't happened. I began to believe in the spirits of Christmas and that one did indeed haunt my bauble.

I returned to the shop on twelfth night. I wasn't entirely surprised to see it was gone. In its place was Marvel's second-hand bookshop. Naturally I went in.

Once again something gorgeous caught my attention. He smiled and I felt dizzy in a way unconnected with my vertigo.

"Hi. Can I help?" he asked.

"Do you have a copy of 'A Christmas Carol'?" Despite telling the previous shopkeeper I didn't believe in the ghosts of Christmas past, present and future I'd never read it. Perhaps it would help me understand?

He produced a beautifully illustrated copy. "Usually it's at home but I dreamed about my grandmother last night. She used to read it to me. Thinking we'd be quiet today I brought it in. Sorry I can't sell it. She made me promise to keep it in the family and give it to my grandkids."

I tried talking him round over coffee. We haggled over dinner. Reached a compromise months later.

One day he'll give the book to his grandchildren. Now though, as I hang my gorgeous Christmas bauble in the window, where it will catch the light, he's upstairs reading 'A Christmas Carol' to our son.

17. The Face On The Floor

As Harriet stepped onto the bathroom scales her attention was caught by something moving on the floor. Not another spider; it looked like a wisp of steam. It was there such a short time she wasn't sure she'd really seen it. When it was gone, Harriet spotted the pattern of a face in her newly installed flooring. It looked disapproving. Why, because of her weight? Or because she was weighing herself and bothered about it? The idea of moving to the country was to get away from silly pressures like that and concentrate on her artwork, but it didn't seem to be working.

Her weight hadn't gone up, despite her regular visits to the village bakery. The effort of restoring Forget-Me-Not cottage was at least burning up calories as well as her bank balance. She told herself to ignore the face, that it was just the pattern of wood grain in the vinyl strips she'd laid in the bathroom and landing. Harriet did try, but as she worked on her home the face looked less and less happy.

Maybe it was just the angle she saw it from. It appeared upside down, almost as though it had deliberately turned away from her. Because of its position against the wall there was no other way to look at it. The pattern would be repeated on other pieces of flooring though and she could examine them from other angles. She studied the floor, but couldn't find it. Odd, it was only a small area though. Maybe that particular strip design wasn't re-used?

Harriet tried to put it from her mind and work, but she

found herself going not towards her studio but to the junk room where the offcuts of flooring were stored in case they might be useful elsewhere. She checked each piece, but found nothing resembling a face. The one in her bathroom was a one off then. A flaw in the floor? Harriet laughed at her own joke. Was she getting hysterical? Maybe not, but she would benefit from company.

Eva, a gallery owner, arrived for the weekend loaded down with wine, bags and gossip. Once Harriet was caught up on all the news from town, and they'd eaten, her friend asked about life in the countryside. "Is it as peaceful as you'd hoped?"

Harriet topped up their wineglasses. "It is, yes. I've had visits from the neighbours, welcoming me to the village, but generally people don't call round unless invited. I haven't got the internet or phone line set up yet and the mobile signal isn't great, so unless I go shopping I might not speak to, or even see, anyone at all for days."

"So you've got scads of work done? Fantastic."

"On the cottage, yes. I've not painted anything except the walls really."

"Ah."

"What's that mean?"

"You don't seem as enthusiastic about this place as I thought you'd be. It really is lovely and exactly what you said you needed, but I guess all the hard work involved is putting a dampener on your imagination."

"Quite the opposite actually." Harriet told her about the grumpy face.

"I don't think that's anything to worry about. It's quite common. Pareidolia I think it's called, seeing faces when we know they're not really there."

"Like seeing Jesus in a crisp?"

"That sort of thing. People see what they want, or expect, to see."

"Must be because I'm feeling a little cut off down here. The neighbours who've come said they'd like to see my paintings of local scenes and I haven't done any, so I've not been in touch. I planned to have lots of visitors from town. I will if I ever finish renovating."

"Yes, of course you will, and you'll make new friends here."

"I'm not so sure. Don't let everyone forget me will you?"

"Don't be daft."

In the morning, Eva came downstairs and said, "I see what you mean about that face. It is a bit alarming. No wonder you're feeling so insecure."

"I'm not." Even so, she was pleased her friend had seen it too.

"No? What was all that stuff about not being forgotten?"

"Did I say that? Must have been the wine talking."

"Maybe. You can always come back and see everyone you know. My sofa is quite comfy, if you remember."

"Thanks, but I really don't have time right now."

"Get some paintings done then will you? I've got customers pestering me for more of your work."

After Eva left, Harriet told herself she must make a determined effort to finish the renovations so she could put it behind her and get on with finding new friends and inviting her old ones to stay, otherwise she really would be forgotten. The face on the bathroom floor stopped looking disapproving and started to seem angry; almost threatening.

She'd taken the wrong approach she decided. She'd come here to work; that's what she should do. If she didn't, then the galleries and critics would certainly forget her. Harriet did try to work, but her paintings were a disaster. There was no excuse. The local scenery was inspirational, she had the peace she craved, and her studio, like the bathroom next to it, got good clear light most of the day. Atmospheric, realistic landscapes were what she was known for. Or had been known for when people could remember who she was. Now she was putting faces in everywhere. No, not faces but the same one over and over. It was that thing in the bathroom.

Harriet strode off to the bathroom. She lifted the scales and placed them decisively over the face. As she stood up a sharp pain burst into her head. She staggered forward to close the blind against the bright sunshine. She stubbed her toe but otherwise felt immediately better. She looked down. As she'd reached to close the window blind she'd knocked the scales away from the face. With her foot she nudged them back into position. Her headache returned. She slid the scales off again and the pain went.

She ran from the bathroom, into the junk room and slammed the door. Why? Why had she come in here? There was a reason she knew. So she wasn't forgotten, that was it. She had to find it so people remembered. Harriet rummaged through boxes. Not her own but ones which had been stored away there for decades. The previous owners told her they'd been there when they moved in and Harriet hadn't got round to looking in them yet. Perhaps she'd find it in there? Whatever 'it' was.

She pulled a couple of boxes off the pile, then pushed her

hand into one she'd uncovered and extracted an old framed photograph. The glass was dirty and the picture faded, but even so the person in it was vaguely familiar. The background she definitely recognised, it was her new home, Forgot-Me-Not cottage. Carefully Harriet removed the picture from the frame and turned it over. There was writing on the back. A name and date she guessed, but it was hard to make out. The year looked like 1858. Photographs would have been rare and expensive back then, so whoever it was clearly wanted to be remembered. Oh.

She recalled her panic as she'd run into the room and her horror of being forgotten. What had all that been about? Slowly Harriet climbed the stairs and went into the bathroom. She opened the blind letting light flood back into the room. The face on the floor was no longer angry or threatening, it just looked sad. So did the one in the photo she realised, now she could see it better. Harriet studied the writing on the back. She was sure she'd been right about the year. The name was possibly Herbert or maybe Hubert, a clear J and then something with E double l for the surname. Elliott? Ellison? No, there was a y at the end. Ellory! She knew that name. If only she had internet access she could look him up. Perhaps she didn't have to though. There was a shop in the village called Ellory's so he must have been local.

Harriet took the photo around to her nearest neighbour to ask if she knew anything about Mr Ellory.

"Hello, dear. Harriet isn't it?"

"That's right. I think you said you've lived here a long time, so I was hoping you could answer a question for me."

"Is it local history you're interested in?"

"I think so."

Her neighbour made tea and offered a slice of home made fruit cake while Harriet explained about the photograph.

"I think the name on the back is Ellory and as there's a local shop by that name I wondered if there was a connection."

"Possibly. The shop has changed hands quite a few times since I've been here, but it kept the name. I think it had to… It's a bit early to call Australia. I'll try later."

"Australia?"

"Yes. My brother lives out there now. He owned Ellory's at one time. I'll find out what I can tonight."

"Thank you."

The sun was low in the sky as Harriet walked home. It lit up Forget-Me-Not cottage with an orange glow, just like an old photo. She wanted to paint it just like that, try to capture the feeling of history in its old walls. She grabbed her pad and sketched until the light was gone. Then she went inside and began transferring the image to a huge canvas. It was a good thing her neighbour had been generous with the cake as Harriet worked without stopping until she was too tired to continue. In the morning she took her cereal and tea into the studio and began working between mouthfuls. She'd not felt like this since she'd moved to the cottage. It was a long time since her work had seemed instinctive instead of deliberate and painstaking. Perhaps she'd never worked with quite such enthusiasm.

Harriet only stopped working to use the bathroom. She looked at the face on the floor, something she'd been avoiding doing as much as possible. It wasn't as clear as it had been, but it looked less miserable. She returned to her studio and studied what she'd done so far. It was good, really good. The cottage looked much as it did now, surrounded by mature trees and with the pots of flowers Harriet had added, but they seemed almost distant compared with the man in the foreground. She hadn't meant to include him, she very rarely painted people, but maybe it wasn't surprising that she had; as well as her sketches, she'd been working from the old photograph. Mr Ellory, because it was him she was painting, looked so real, so hard to miss.

That evening Harriet returned to her neighbour. She knew the lady would be waiting. That she wouldn't have forgotten Harriet, nor her promise to help.

"I was right," she said once they were both sat with tea and cake. "People who bought the shop did have to keep the name. Mr Ellory stated that in his will and there's something in the deeds about it. I wonder why."

"He didn't want to be forgotten."

"That must be the answer and it explains the name of your cottage. It's been called Forget-Me-Not cottage since he built it."

Harriet worked for days, stopping only to eat and sleep. While she waited for the oils to dry she started other smaller pictures of local scenes. This time no unwanted elements appeared in her work. As her pictures took shape she became happier and happier. Odd that she'd not realised how miserable she'd been before. Odd too about the face on the floor. Day by day it grew fainter. Day by day its scowl lessened.

When the painting of her cottage was finished Harriet phoned Eva. "You'll be pleased to know I've been working like crazy."

"So the restorations are finished?"

"No, the cottage is no further forward than when you were

here. I've been painting."

"I'm coming down."

Eva arrived the next morning.

"Put the kettle on will you? I've finished but I need to clean up," Harriet said.

"That can wait. Show me the pictures."

Eva stared at Harriet's new work. She didn't speak for several long minutes as she examined each one carefully, returning often to the one of Mr Ellory outside the cottage.

"Harriet, if you don't sell me every one of these I'll never speak to you again."

"The big one isn't for sale."

"I have to have it for the gallery. Absolutely have to."

"You can display it, but I'm not selling. I don't want it shut away unseen in a private collection."

"You're right,it should be seen. OK it's a deal."

Harriet went into the bathroom to clean up.

"I've finished painting you, Mr Ellory," she said to the floor. "It's my best work and will hang in a big gallery. Thousands of people will see it and they'll step forward to see the title and read Hubert J Ellory of Forget-Me-Not cottage. You won't be forgotten, I promise."

The face on the floor smiled then swirled for a moment like a wisp of steam. Once it was still again, the face was gone and all Harriet could see was the pattern of wood grain.

18. Every Cloud

Raina had never had any luck, starting from when she'd been given her name. It was frequently misspelled. She'd had trouble with just about every legal document she'd applied for. Even one of her wedding photos revealed a worried frown as she double-checked the marriage certificate.

"It means baby or queen," Gran had told her once. "It's perfect as you're our little princess."

Appropriately Raina now lived in a palatial home. The once grand house was divided into flats. After years of study and hard work she was mortgaged up to the ears for the smallest and shabbiest of these and had to spend all her free time making it fit to live in. Until then, she was sleeping on Gran's sofa.

At school she'd been nicknamed Rainy.

"People still do it," she complained to Gran.

"That's probably because of the dark cloud you insist on sitting under. You never look on the bright side."

Raina had denied it, but not felt optimistic when Gran said she'd got one of the new five pound notes for each of her grandchildren.

"I saw on the news that some of them are worth thousands," she'd said excitedly.

Raina checked the serial numbers and discovered there was no hope of one paying for someone else to renovate her flat.

"I know it's not worth a fortune, but in a way it's part of history," Gran said.

"That's true. Thanks, Gran. I'd better get going; I've got woodwork to sand and walls to prepare."

Raina was beyond fed up by the time she began stripping paper from the last wall. That was until she discovered a tiny door. With renewed energy she soaked and scraped at the decades worth of layers until she could prise it open. It revealed a small compartment hidden behind the skirting. Raina fetched a torch and cautiously reached inside.

The contents proved to be messages from people who'd opened the compartment before. The first was hard to read. It was as old as the building and the words were poorly formed with most incorrectly spelled. The writer said he'd been trying to get a labouring job there when the owner's daughter came to look round. She'd dropped a brooch which, although tempted to keep, he'd returned to the young lady. His reward was a shilling and a better job than he'd ever dreamed of. He was being trained as a carpenter and had made the compartment as practice. Whoever found it would be another worker like him and he'd wanted to pass on his luck, so left the shilling.

The next letter Raina read had been written soon after the Great War. The workman wrote he was lucky to have survived when so many hadn't, and lucky too that able-bodied men were now so scarce they earned good wages. He felt guilty enough profiting from that, so added his medal to the shilling.

One note, undated but written on a very old envelope with the early stamp intact, said the writer had nothing valuable to add, as all his money was sent home to his family, but he was grateful to be strong and skilled enough to support them. He hoped to see them soon.

The final letter was written by a man who'd been involved in converting the house into flats. He'd just had a son. Such good luck was enough for him, he didn't need hidden treasure. He'd replaced the shilling and medal, named the child after the war hero and added one of the toys being made in the nearby, newly opened, factory.

Raina reached further inside the compartment and discovered a small box with 'Meccano Dinky Toys' printed on the label.

Treasure seemed exactly the right word for the haul she'd uncovered. Its value to Raina though wasn't something to be calculated in pounds. As she read she'd realised how lucky she was not to know the horror of war, to have had an education which led to a job she loved and didn't rely on her staying strong in order to have food and a roof over her head. She was fortunate that although her husband was working away, she could speak to him every day.

She wrote her own letter explaining all that, added it and her five pound note and sealed everything back into the compartment. Then she went to tell her gran what she'd done and how she'd finally noticed her cloud had a brilliant silver lining.

19. Wilma's Warning

Sarah had always envied Wilma. She wasn't alone in that, many of her classmates did too. It wasn't for her looks exactly, but for her signature look. Even though this constantly changed, there was always something about it that was essentially Wilma.

Like Sarah, Wilma was small and naturally nondescript. Unlike Sarah, the older girl wasn't content with that and stood out in so many ways. Her version of school uniform might land her in detention now and then, but it actually looked good. Totally unlike the frumpy outfit Sarah was forced to wear because her boring parents insisted on sticking to every rule, no matter how dorky it made their daughter look. Sarah's hair was pulled into a neat ponytail. Wilma's was always styled and coloured.

The only good thing about the dreaded Monday mornings was seeing what new look Wilma had created over the weekend. Tuesdays were of some interest as Sarah got to see how others interpreted Wilma's new look and tried to copy it. Seeing how badly some failed only partially made up for the fact that Sarah was never allowed to make the attempt.

Wilma always wore a big brooch, in the shape of a spooky, spiky letter W. Sarah and several others tried to get something similar. Brooches in the shape of their initials were easy to find, but were smooth, pretty and safe. They were poor imitations of the only thing constant about Wilma's appearance.

Sarah wasn't friends with Wilma. She was too young and boring to interest such a girl. At least she guessed that's how she'd be seen and was usually too timid to approach her. One day, when Wilma's hair was a particularly vivid orange and sculpted into dramatic curls, Sarah managed to say, "Great colour."

Wilma had actually stopped and spoken to her! "You could do yours the same." She'd even told her which shade of dye she'd used, but of course Sarah's mum wouldn't let her try.

"The school says no hair dye and no make-up," she'd said. A tinted lip gloss was the most Sarah was allowed Monday to Friday, and not much more at the weekend. She did wear more obviously, but had to put it on after she left the house and try to remember to remove it before coming home.

Dad was always reading things out of the paper in an attempt to scare her into toeing the line. Every report of homelessness, medical problems or theft came with the dire warning 'that could be you' if she didn't pay attention at school, eat her greens and keep her phone out of sight.

Sarah tried to point out the times taking a risk had paid off. The kid who skived off school to watch a TV show being recorded, somehow got himself into shot and eventually ended up with an acting career. Entrepreneurs gambling their homes to set up cool new businesses. Groundbreaking medical techniques started as experiments and now saving lives. It didn't help. Such examples were rare and the last one reminded Dad of a recent case where a too trusting nurse was arrested along with a doctor who'd carried out deadly, illegal research. If her alibi of being innocently sleeping at her parent's home hadn't been believed, the nurse would have received a sentence of life imprisonment. Dad read that last fact twice.

Wilma's parents must be less rigid than Sarah's. Less keen for their daughter to be a boring nobody, as even her name was cool and distinctive. Half of Sarah's class shared a name with at least one of the other girls. There were six Emmas, four Emilys, five Kaitlyns and three other Sarahs just in her year, but only one Wilma in the whole school.

Every fun or daring thing which happened at school, from filling the stationery cupboard with fire extinguisher foam, through sponsored, spoonless jelly eating, to the cat in Miss Jenkins' desk, involved Wilma. Once, when on an errand for a teacher, Sarah had seen Wilma sneaking down the corridor towards the headteacher's landing. She'd beckoned Sarah to join her. Sarah had hurried on, unsure if she'd really seen that gesture and pretending she hadn't.

Teachers attempted to use Wilma as a warning. Pay attention, do your homework, don't roll up the waistband on your skirt or you'll seem like Wilma. It didn't work. Not before Wilma was expelled and not afterwards. When that happened, Sarah was desperate to do something daring enough to earn the reward of freedom from stupid rules forever. Her parents would have none of it.

Mum and Dad literally policed everything she wore, inspected the contents of her school bag and stood over her to ensure she did her homework. They stopped giving her money for the bus and food and instead took it in turns to take her, plus a packed lunch, right to the gate. It was so unfair!

"Look at this, love. This is why there are rules you must follow," Dad said one day, showing her the local paper.

'Local girl missing' the headline said.

It was Wilma they were talking about. She'd stormed out

the family home after a row and not been seen again. Apparently no one knew what had happened to her. Sarah couldn't help speculating. Maybe a talent scout spotted her and she'd gone to work as a model? Maybe she was fruit picking in the Spanish sun? Or perhaps she'd fallen in love with one of the travellers who'd been living on the common and gone with him when they moved on? Whatever it was, it would be something fun and exciting. Whatever it was, she'd left without a trace.

Sarah's parents became stricter after that. It was like living in lockdown and Sarah rebelled. One night, after a row, she did everything they told her not to, including going out without telling them where, drinking alcohol and talking to strangers. Well, one stranger actually. A woman; Sarah wasn't a complete idiot. She'd said no to the boys who'd flirted and offered drinks, but accepted when the woman gestured for her to come over. In fact at first Sarah hadn't realised she was a stranger, as her smiling face looked reassuringly familiar.

"You won't get bothered if you're not on your own," she said, in a voice Sarah was sure she didn't recognise.

The woman was amusing, generous and treated her like an adult. It was she who bought Sarah the vodka and Coke. It just tasted like Coke, which was a little disappointing, but she'd heard it was what Wilma drank and it made her feel brave.

"Do you like wine?" the woman asked.

"Of course," said Sarah, who'd never tried it. What was the woman's name? Sarah couldn't remember if she'd told her and it now seemed too late to ask.

"I have a bottle at home. Want to come back and share it, or do you have to get home?"

Sarah checked her watch. If she left right then and went straight home, she'd just about make her usual curfew. It wouldn't matter though. Mum and Dad would still moan at her for breaking all their other pathetic rules.

"Sure," she said.

On the drive there, Sarah made sure to notice where they were going. Her new friend might invite her to come back another time and she'd look stupid saying, "Um, whatever your name is, can you give me the address of the place I've just spent the evening?"

As Sarah stepped into the woman's house it felt as though two small hands were pushing her away. As Sarah walked down the untidy hallway, it felt like something was clutching at her, trying to drag her back onto the street. She was being silly. Probably just her parents' nagging playing on her mind. She giggled as she imagined them coming round and telling the woman to put her shoes and things away properly.

"You make yourself comfortable," the woman said, gesturing to the lounge. "I'll open the wine."

Sarah attempted to follow the instruction, but felt those hands on her, pushing her back into the hallway. She stumbled and dislodged the jumble of discarded footwear. That's when she saw it; Wilma's W shaped brooch. She never took it off. Not ever. Her insistence on wearing it even when doing PE had been the cause of more than one detention.

"Not thinking of running out on me, were you?" the woman asked.

"Of course not. I just need the bathroom. Is it upstairs?" Sarah spoke the words, but had no idea where they were coming from.

"First door on the left."

"I won't be a minute. Why don't you put some music on?" Sarah gave her what she hoped was a trusting smile. The kind Wilma might have given her, when she'd thought buying vodka for a schoolgirl was the worst she'd do. The kind which had come naturally to Sarah until she'd realised why the woman looked familiar. She was the nurse from Dad's paper. Clearly it had been the jury who were too trusting, not the renegade doctor's innocent looking accomplice.

As Sarah went upstairs, she felt those ghostly hands again. This time they were pushing her on, not holding her back. When she reached the bathroom, they seemed to guide Sarah's fingers first to the bolt on the door, then to the keypad of her phone.

"Sarah, where the hell are you?" Mum shrieked. Then, more gently, "Are you OK, love?

"No! Please just come and get me! I'm at 42a Shipton Street. And, Mum, bring the police."

20. Ghostly Goings On At Gran's House

Chloe stood on the pavement looking at Gran's house. After her funeral, family and friends had gathered there to celebrate her long and happy life, yet somehow it didn't feel as though Gran was really gone.

"Back again?" asked an attractively deep voice.

"Hi, Matt. Seems I can't keep away." She gave a bright smile to the man who was part of her reason for being there.

Something warm and wet touched her hand.

"Harvey! Down!" Mat commanded.

Chloe bent to make a fuss of the fat little dog. She liked Harvey and, from the way he wagged his tail and always leapt up to lick her hand, knew he liked her too. The feelings between her and Matt were a lot less clear. He'd been born in Gran's road, so they'd known each other as children, but they hadn't really been friends.

"Give him a chance," Gran had said more than once.

Chloe had realised he was shy, and didn't mind when her cousins invited him to play, but hadn't bothered making much effort at friendship herself. Just when she was old enough to appreciate a good looking boy with broad shoulders and quiet, gentle manner he'd moved away. He often visited his parents, Gran said, but that had rarely coincided with Chloe's own visits to Gran. Matt and Chloe had bumped into each other roughly once a year. In the meantime Gran had updated her on his various jobs, the fact he was still single, that his parents were emigrating and he'd returned to his childhood home. Probably matchmaking attempts would have followed, had Gran lived long enough.

Chloe and her cousins had inherited Gran's house and decided to let it out. One, an electrician, replaced the wiring. That was something Gran had said wasn't worth the disruption and which he claimed he'd never have started if he'd known the house was haunted. The others paid for further renovations. They didn't change more than they had to. The hooks where Gran had hung coats, picture rails, even the cat-flap for the long gone Tabatha remained. They kept some of her furniture too; the kitchen table, chairs and dresser fitted the house so well it felt wrong to remove them. Chloe's task was decorating, something she enjoyed.

Matt had walked by with Harvey several times as she was doing the work. They said 'hello' but didn't get much beyond that until one day he'd passed as she was unloading wallpaper and paint from her car.

"Are you moving in?" he'd asked.

Maybe it was her imagination, but she'd thought he sounded hopeful. As she'd looked into those hard-to-read grey eyes, she regretted she hadn't done as Gran asked and given him the chance to become a proper friend.

"Sadly not," she'd said.

"That's a shame," he'd said, then he and Harvey were off.

They continued in that manner for quite a while. Matt spoke to Chloe whenever he saw her, but only for a moment then he'd gently tug on Harvey's lead and they'd disappear up the road. Matt almost always seemed to go by just after she'd parked outside Gran's house. Maybe little Harvey and his stubby legs really did need a lot of exercise, but Chloe couldn't help guessing he was more likely to get a walk if

Matt had seen her turning her car at the end of the close.

Remembering Gran telling her to give him a chance, Chloe was very friendly to Matt. She always responded to his greetings and tried to make further conversation. OK, so the way his eyes crinkled when he smiled, the fact his deep voice seemed to warm her from the inside and that he looked big and strong enough to wrap his arms around her and keep her safe from anything, might have had something to do with it too.

Being alone in Gran's house wasn't sad or scary, but there was something odd about it. Often, when she was decorating, she found it hard to concentrate on her task and would find herself remembering time spent there with Gran, or thinking about Matt. Both were understandable, but Chloe wasn't usually a daydreamer. Several times she thought she'd forgotten to finish the lunch she'd brought with her, but the box was always empty so she must have eaten it without realising. Unlike her electrician cousin she didn't believe in ghosts, but sometimes had the weirdest feeling she wasn't alone. The sensation wasn't sinister, but Chloe ensured she locked the doors and kept the downstairs windows closed, so nobody could come in and surprise her as she worked.

Chloe had always loved the house, but it took weeks of applying paint and paper in her favourite colours every weekend, exchanging greetings with Matt and fussing over Harvey, before she decided she should be the one to rent Gran's house.

As Chloe pushed and pulled the 'to let' sign, attempting to remove it, she wasn't really surprised to discover Harvey jumping eagerly up the post, nor Matt giving more practical assistance.

"You've got a tenant then?" Matt asked.

"In a way. I'm your new neighbour," she said offering her hand.

"That's great!" He seemed to mean it, but after the briefest handshake, he and Harvey were off.

He reappeared each time she arrived with the boxes she brought over from her flat and helped carry them in.

The other neighbours all seemed fairly pleasant, although the lady next door warned her to watch out for, "The young man with the dog at number seven. He's so badly behaved."

Chloe wasn't sure if the wrongdoer was Matt or Harvey. Both seemed equally unlikely, especially as she also claimed the government were spying on her.

As well as a fifth share of the house, Chloe had inherited some of Gran's recipe books and cooking equipment. It seemed only right to put them to use and make Gran's legendary oat biscuits. At the side of the recipe there was a note in Gran's tiny writing, 'double the quantities at least!' Chloe smiled as she remembered the times she and her cousins had eaten the entire batch. Gran always pretended to think they'd vanished into thin air – and made more. Chloe made only a small quantity of biscuits. They smelled just like Gran's had. She was eager to taste them and in order to stop herself doing that before they were cool, went upstairs to have a shower.

The smell of baking flooded through the house and added to the comforting feeling she wasn't alone. That sensation wasn't so pleasant when she discovered her biscuits had vanished.

She quickly established that the doors were still locked, the windows closed. The empty cooling rack didn't seem to be quite in the same place and Chloe wasn't certain if she'd left the kitchen chair pulled out like that, but otherwise there was no sign anyone had been in the house. It was so odd. Chloe was tired and moving home is always stressful, plus she was still grieving for Gran. Maybe she'd eaten them before her shower without noticing? After all, she'd done that with her lunch while she was decorating, hadn't she?

The next week Chloe baked another batch of biscuits; vanilla swirls this time. She was going to eat those, and she was going to enjoy them, not polish off the lot without noticing. Maybe she shouldn't wait for them to cool? She was just reaching for one, when the phone rang. The call was from a friend she'd not spoken to for a while. By the time they were caught up on each other's news, Chloe was more than ready for a snack.

Once again the biscuits had vanished. Chloe couldn't have eaten them herself; she was really hungry. She'd put the wire rack in the middle of the table, now it was at the end and the tea towel she'd covered it with was on a kitchen chair. Nothing else was missing and there was no sign of a break in. Was her cousin right about the house being haunted? Surely if there was a ghost it had to be Gran? If it was, what message could she be trying to give? The only thing Chloe could think of was that Gran wanted her to bake more biscuits, so she did.

The next lot vanished too, but there was nothing ghostly about that. She'd heard Matt talking to Harvey and opened the front door just as he was at the end of her path.

"I've just made ginger biscuits, would you like one?"

She thought he was going to refuse, but Harvey pulled on the lead and Matt followed him into the house. He stood awkwardly in her kitchen, reminding Chloe of the little boy who'd hung around but rarely spoken to her. It seemed he hadn't entirely lost his shyness.

Chloe chattered as she filled the kettle and set out mugs, trying to get him talking.

"Do you take milk?"

"Yes please."

"How about sugar?"

"No thanks."

"The weather has been lovely today, hasn't it?"

"Warm, yes."

"They say it's going to break soon though. What do you think?"

"It could rain."

She kept going, but three words was his longest answer and, "These are delicious," his only unprompted remark, until she asked if Harvey would like a biscuit. It was a daft question as the little dog had pounced on a dropped crumb and was clearly hoping for more.

"He would, but I'd rather you didn't give him any. He's getting a bit podgy and I've put the poor little chap on a diet. He doesn't like it."

From the way Harvey was licking the floor where another crumb had fallen, Chloe could easily believe that.

"I'll eat his, if you don't mind?" Matt said, reaching for a sixth biscuit.

Once Matt had started talking, he didn't seem to find it so difficult to keep going. In fact he began a conversation about the garden. By the time he and Harvey left, Matt had eaten the last of Chloe's biscuits and offered to come round and make her rickety fence more secure.

Nothing else odd happened for two days, then one morning Chloe found Gran's cookbook open on the kitchen table. She was almost sure she hadn't left it there, but she had realised Matt was fond of home baking and been thinking of cooking something nice to thank him for fixing the fence. The open page was for individual lemon cakes and had another note in Gran's tiny writing. Did that say 'Matt's favourite'?

Chloe rang her cousin to ask about the ghostly experience he claimed to have had. Not because she believed Gran was nipping out of the spirit world to eat biscuits or offer recipe suggestions, but in the hope it would offer clues as to what was really happening.

"What was it you thought vanished?"

"What are you on about, Chloe? Nothing vanished."

"What happened then?"

"I probably just got spooked being in Gran's house on my own so soon after… after we lost her. But, well, a few times I thought there was someone there."

"That's it?"

"It was enough for me! Why do you ask?"

"Things have gone missing or I've found them where they shouldn't be."

Her cousin laughed. "That's not ghosts, it's just that you're used to your tiny flat where everything was in sight and now you've got space to lose things."

Chloe tried to believe him and made a trial batch of the lemon cakes. None disappeared between being left to cool and Chloe topping them with buttercream. One vanished immediately afterwards; into her mouth. It tasted wonderful. The girls at work thought so too when she took in those she hadn't eaten.

When she made the batch to share with Matt, she made

the mistake of doing so just before lunch. When she came to ice them only nine of the original twelve remained. Chloe knew she'd given in to temptation and eaten one, but was almost positive it had only been the one.

She didn't intend to say anything about it to Matt, but once he'd done what he could with the fence she offered the tea and cakes. "That's if there's any left."

"I thought you lived alone?"

"So did I! I mean, of course I do… I was starting to think there might be a poltergeist or something, but my cousin said it's just that I'm not used to living in a house on my own."

"That can be unsettling. When I first moved into Mum and Dad's place, after they went to Spain, it felt so strange. All the night time creaks I'd grown up with suddenly sounded sinister. Then I got Harvey."

"And everything was fine?"

Matt chuckled. "Not exactly. He was a bit of a terror and was always escaping. He's almost got over it now, but at one time I couldn't open a door without him flying out and doing a lap of the close."

"Ah, that explains the lady next door saying he was badly behaved."

"He has got into her garden a couple of times… Oh no! Where is he?"

"He was just here and you've fixed the fence so he can't have got out." This was horrible. Vanishing food was odd, but anything happening to Harvey would be awful.

"Harvey! Harvey, come here boy," Matt called.

There was a clunk and Harvey tumbled out of the cat-flap in Chloe's kitchen door, licking buttercream from his face.

"Oh, Chloe I'm so sorry! He can be incredibly athletic if it means getting extra grub. Looks like he's eaten your cakes."

She laughed with relief. "And not for the first time. Harvey is my poltergeist."

"I'm so, so sorry. He still escapes occasionally and always heads straight for your house. I think your Gran gave him titbits though she always denied it. I didn't realise… I don't know what to say."

"I do. Matt, will you come out with me sometime?"

Matt looked totally stunned for a moment. Then horribly embarrassed.

She'd been an idiot. Yes he was shy, but she had no reason to suppose that was the only thing stopping him from asking her out. She'd hoped him always appearing whenever she arrived at the house was because he wanted to talk to her, but probably he really was just walking Harvey, or taking him home after he'd escaped.

"You'd really go out with me?" he asked.

"Yes, Matt. Tomorrow night? Pick me up at seven-thirty?"

He grinned, blushed and nodded.

Chloe heard a sound exactly like Gran saying 'at last'. It must just have been the wind, or someone's TV, because she there was no such thing as ghosts. Four legged cupids though, they were definitely real. She'd bake a new batch of cookies, this time with all dog friendly ingredients, for Harvey to munch while she and Matt were out. It wouldn't help his diet, but cupids are supposed to be chubby, aren't they?

21. Matt's Shadow

Matt watched as his shadow wobbled, then lifted its hand. Clutched between its fingers was the heavy paperweight from Miss Price's desk. Matt hadn't seen the shadow take that, but it must have snatched it when he'd helped put the books away. Luckily Miss was writing on the board so couldn't see the shadow waving its trophy in the air. It was nearly home time so Matt could probably put it back on his way out and Miss would never know.

"Please put it down," he begged, though quietly so Miss Price didn't hear.

The shadow must have heard, but of course it took no notice of him. It rarely did.

"Put it down now!" He hissed the words.

The shadow's arm moved back. With horror Matt saw it was preparing to throw.

"No, please no," he said.

It didn't help. The shadow threw the paperweight at the window.

Matt ran. It seemed to him he was out the classroom and down the corridor before he heard the crash of breaking glass. He couldn't run fast enough to avoid hearing his name called. Miss Price's angry voice reached the shadow first; it ran on ahead of Matt. Of course it did. The shadow caused the trouble, Matt took the blame. Every time.

Maybe he was to blame? He'd shouted at it only that

morning when it had refused to wave goodbye to Mum after she dropped him at school. Shouting made the shadow stronger, nastier. Stood to reason. It had just been an ordinary shadow before the rows. One just like anyone else's, which followed him and did what he did.

When his parents began arguing it started to go wobbly and behave badly. It stole sweets from the local shop, but so far only Matt had noticed. When it refused to pick up toys, wouldn't eat properly, stayed in his bedroom instead of watching TV in the lounge and cried at night instead of going to sleep, Mum and Dad noticed. They didn't know it was the shadow's fault. Mum said it was Dad's fault.

Dad had yelled, "That's right, everything that goes wrong is always my fault."

Matt didn't think Dad had meant it. He never said sorry or tried to be nice to make it all right.

Miss Price noticed when the shadow wouldn't sit still in class, when it pulled people's hair or knocked their work off desks. Last week she had a talk with Matt, saying it wasn't fair on the others to disrupt classes or spoil their work.

"No, Miss. It isn't fair." It wasn't fair the shadow did it, or that Matt got the blame.

She asked him why he did it.

"It's not me," he'd said.

She didn't say so, but he could tell she hadn't believed him. Why do grown ups not say what the mean and mean what they say?

"Is there anything worrying you, Matt?" Miss Price asked.

Matt wanted to tell her but he was sure the shadow was trying to poke out its tongue so he kept his mouth shut tight.

"I'm going to have to speak to your parents about your

behaviour."

Matt and his shadow both shrugged. Matt didn't think his parents would tell him off; they were always too busy shouting at each other to even talk to him. He knew the shadow wouldn't get into trouble.

Matt was right; he heard them arguing about him.

Dad said, "It's your fault, you're too soft on him. You're always buying him sweets and things when we can barely afford the food he won't eat."

"I do not! I don't know where he gets them all from. I am surprised you've noticed though; you're never here!"

"I'm trying to keep a roof over our heads, but I don't suppose you've noticed that!"

Dad put bags and boxes into his car and drove away saying he'd see Matt at the weekend. That was yesterday. Today the shadow had broken a window in Miss Price's classroom.

Matt and his shadow ran down the corridor, past Mrs Jennings' class, with the shadow racing ahead. Miss Price and Mrs Jennings called for him to wait, but Matt just ran. The shadow rushed out of the school, across the grass, through the hole in the hedge and onto the street.

Matt followed, seeing nothing but the shadow. It went into the road where a car hit it. The shadow flew into the air, then fell back down. For a moment everything went black. Then Matt saw lots of faces all looking at him. He heard lots of voices talking to him but they didn't make sense until he heard Miss Price.

"I'm his teacher and first aid trained. Please all stand back."

Miss Price asked him if he knew who she was.

"Yes, Miss Price."

"Do you know where you are?"

"In the road outside school."

"Does it hurt anywhere?"

"Yes, Miss." He started to cry then. Everything hurt, especially his arm. He tried to lift it to see if there was anything wrong with it, but that made him feel sick. Everything got dark again.

When he opened his eyes again he was somewhere else and Miss Price was holding the hand of the arm which didn't hurt so much.

"You're in an ambulance, Matt and you're going to hospital. I telephoned your Mum and she's on the way to the hospital now. You'll be just fine soon."

He wasn't sure if she meant that as her voice was all wobbly, just like the shadow was before it did something bad.

"Will I die, Miss?"

"No, Matt. You might have to have an operation on your arm though. That won't be very nice, but you'll be fine afterwards."

She did mean that.

At the hospital lots of different people came and looked at him. They wheeled him about on a bed and sometimes Miss Price had to run to keep up. Matt couldn't tell if the shadow was there too as he was looking up all the time. A man told him about the operation that might be done on his arm. It was broken but they could sort of bolt it back together again. It sounded odd, but the man said it wouldn't hurt. Matt liked the man, he seemed like he'd only ever say what he meant and he'd always mean what he said.

"You'll have some impressive scars and will have to come back to hospital, but you and that arm of yours will be good as new long before you get to secondary school."

Matt smiled. The shadow wouldn't have any scars at all, but Matt would have really good ones.

Sometimes Matt and Miss Price were on their own.

"Do you want to talk, Matt?"

He could imagine the shadow shaking its head, but he still couldn't see it. Matt didn't shake his head; moving hurt his arm so he stayed still and looked at Miss Price. He told her all about the shadow and the bad things it had done, about Mum and Dad rowing and about Dad going away. And he told her about grownups not always saying what they meant.

"Oh, Matt I didn't know," Miss Price said.

Matt thought he heard Mum's voice, but felt really tired and had to close his eyes for a while. When he opened them again Mum was there. She didn't shout at anyone.

She kissed him and said, "Matt it's me, Mum."

"I know, Mum."

"You're going to have an operation."

"I know."

She kissed him again. "I love you."

He didn't say 'I know' because he wouldn't have meant it. Instead he said, "Love you too."

Some men came and one said, "Time to go, Matt."

Miss Price squeezed his hand and said she'd come and see him later, then Matt was wheeled away. Mum came with him. He couldn't see the shadow, because he was still looking up.

They went down some corridors then one of the men

pushing Matt's bed said, "This is it. Don't worry, he'll be fine." He said it to Mum not to Matt, because Matt already knew.

Mum kissed him again and said she loved him. Then Matt was wheeled away from her.

"Matt!" It was Dad's voice yelling, but not like he was angry.

"Wait!" Mum shouted. "Please wait, his dad is coming."

Matt's bed stopped moving.

Dad kissed him and said, "Love you, Son."

"Love you too, Dad."

Then Matt's bed was pushed into a room and the men who'd done the pushing lifted him on to the bed and said. "See you later."

There were people there with masks on their faces, just like the man who said what he meant had told him. A lady gave Matt an injection and it went all dark again.

When he woke up Mum and Dad were both there. He felt sick and kept going to sleep that day, but one of them was always there when he woke up, even when it was night. They were both there the next day when he felt better and could get out of bed. His shadow was there too. It was wobbly, but then so was Matt. He thought it wobbled just the same way he did, but he tried not to look at it much, just in case.

Mum and Dad talked to him a lot. They talked about his arm and about the rows and they said they'd talked to Miss Price too.

Dad said, "You are right that people don't always mean what they say and your Mum and I have said horrible things to each other that we didn't really mean."

"Are you going to be at home when I get out of hospital?"

"Yes." His voice sounded wobbly.

Matt stood up and walked a few steps away. He saw a dark shape move on the wall. He thought it might be his shadow so he looked at Mum instead.

"Matt your dad has come back home for now, but we don't know if he will be staying with us all the time. We are going to try to get along, but neither of us can promise that it will work out."

"We do promise not to shout at each other or say nasty things," Dad said. "And we'll both always love you, whatever happens."

Matt nodded his head. So did the shadow. Mum and Dad's shadows appeared either side of his, then got closer as his parents gently hugged him. The shadow turned into one great big one, then back into three smaller ones again when they moved apart. They didn't wobble.

22. Crushed Apples

After a rare night out with friends, Joanna was heading home as quickly as she dared on the slippery pavement. Normally, no matter what the weather, the High Street paths provided plenty of grip, but that night it felt as though something soft was smeared underfoot. Joanna wondered if someone had spilled detergent, but didn't stop to investigate. It was gone eleven and raining heavily; she wanted to be home before her husband started to worry.

Joanna pulled her hood down with one hand as she scurried down the long High Street into another gust of cold wind. With it came a strong aroma of apples. The combination of the smell, similar weather conditions, and knowing Mike was waiting, reminded Joanna of an incident which happened nearly thirty years previously. She'd just started dating Mike and been on her way to meet him, when she'd passed an elderly woman scraping up fallen apples. She was filling a wheelbarrow with whole and crushed fruit.

"Perhaps you should leave that and get inside?" Joanna had suggested.

"I daren't. The pavement has got so slippery with people treading on them, and now all the rain. Someone might get hurt."

Joanna felt the only danger was to the sweet old lady, but as helping seemed the quickest way to get her out of the awful weather, Joanna shovelled up windfall fruit, lugged the barrow into the lady's garden, and urged her to go inside.

"Will you come in for a cup of tea?" she'd offered. "I'll put on the fire and you can dry yourself off."

"No thanks. My boyfriend will be waiting for me."

"Oh dear, and I've held you up! I must repay your kindness," the lady said.

"No, really, it's OK. It only took a few minutes."

"A small amount of time, but it's made a big difference."

Mike had looked grumpy when Joanna arrived, slightly later than the time they'd agreed.

"I've paid for the whole film, I don't want to miss any of it." But then he'd noticed how wet and cold she was, and that there was apple pulp on her jeans. He wrapped his warm scarf around her neck. "Are you OK? Did you fall over?"

"Sort of the opposite." She explained about helping the old woman. "She was really pleased and wanted to repay me."

Mike brightened up. "And she lives in one of those big houses on Holly Avenue? Maybe she'll give you a valuable antique."

"Don't be daft, Mike. She just meant with a cup of tea or something."

"You could call in for it tomorrow. Wouldn't take you long to get round her; you might even end up in her will!"

"Mike!"

"Just a joke. Seriously though, it is worth going back. She'll feel better if she can thank you properly."

Joanna hadn't visited the lady. Mike's comments had made her feel uncomfortable about doing that. Of course he was only joking, but Joanna didn't want the lady to feel she expected a reward. That was all so long ago now.

Another strong waft of apple scent made Joanna stop and look round for the cause. She was nowhere near the greengrocer's and there were no fruit trees in the High Street.

"Please, could you help me?"

Joanna turned to look in the direction the voice had come from and saw she'd walked straight by a woman without noticing her. For a moment Joanna thought it was the lady she'd helped clear fallen apples, but it couldn't be. She'd be over a hundred now and this lady was decades off that. It was probably just because she was dressed the same way, in a long, pale green waterproof coat and matching rain hat, that she appeared so similar.

"What's wrong?" Joanna asked.

"I've dropped my key."

As Joanna searched the pavement which was shiny with rain, the lady explained how it had slipped through her fingers as she tried to open the door leading to her flat.

"I've got it!" Joanna declared. "Shall I unlock for you?"

"You're so very kind."

"Not at all, it's only taken a minute."

"A small amount of time, but it's made a big difference."

How odd! That was just what the other lady had said all those years ago.

Joanna tugged her hood into place once more and hurried towards home. It was too late to protect her hair, but if she stopped the hood being blown back again, she might at least prevent cold rainwater trickling down her neck. In a way Joanna was pleased Mike had declared the fashionable faux fur jacket she'd bought was a waste of money and made her return it. If he hadn't she'd probably have worn it that evening and be completely soaked by now.

Of course if he'd come and picked her up she'd be warm and dry, but she hadn't known how long the meal would go on for. That, his complaints about how much the evening out might cost, and suggestion that as a non-drinker she shouldn't pay an equal share, prompted Joanna to say she'd make her own way home. Joanna could drive but, as she now walked to work, rarely needed to and had agreed with Mike it wasn't worth keeping her own car.

"You'll put me on the insurance policy for yours, won't you?" she'd asked.

"When I renew it."

Perhaps she should have arranged something herself, but when Mike explained in lengthy detail about their various policies, she hadn't followed it all and just signed where he asked her to.

Talking with her old friends that evening had made her see every marriage had its good and bad points. Mike might be a bit 'careful' when it came to money but he didn't cheat on her, drink to excess or get seriously bad tempered. He was quite good at DIY, always put the bins out and often did the washing up.

Some of her old friends went to great lengths to look just as they had in their twenties, so their husband's weren't tempted to look elsewhere. Mike never made her feel insecure like that.

"You look like a real woman, not some painted doll," he'd reassured her before she'd left home that evening.

A noise like an explosion came from the far end of the High Street, stopping Joanna's thoughts instantly. The sound seemed to bounce around between the shops, and rang in her ears. Once everything was quiet again, she walked on cautiously. Soon she was picking her way through slivers of glass. No alarms were ringing and no shop windows looked broken.

It took Joanna a few moments to realise that an illuminated shop sign had crashed down onto the pavement ahead of her. If she hadn't stopped to find that old lady's key, and so been delayed by a minute or so, she'd have reached the spot about when the sign fell. Possibly that exact moment. She could easily have been seriously injured, perhaps killed!

Shaken, she called Mike.

"Have you called an ambulance and the police?" he asked.

"I'm not hurt, but maybe I'd better call the police so they can make sure nobody falls over the sign. You'll come and get me, won't you?"

"Of course. Wait right where you are."

Joanna rang the police, then waited, thinking about what had just happened. 'A small amount of time, but it's made a big difference,' the old lady had said. She hadn't known how true that was… had she? It was odd that two women who looked the same both used those words after Joanna helped them. The first had wanted to repay her kindness. Joanna hadn't seen the second lady until she smelled apples. She lived in a flat that Joanna, who walked past every day, hadn't realised existed. And her dropping a key might have saved Joanna's life.

Mike was there in minutes and leapt out to check her for injuries.

"I told you, I'm not hurt, just shaken up."

Her legs began to tremble and he only just stopped her

sinking to the ground. After helping Joanna into the car, Mike asked if she'd got an incident number from the police.

"I didn't ask. Should I have done?"

"No, no. It's natural you weren't thinking of details like that. Don't worry, I'll call and get it tomorrow."

He left her in the car, with the heating on full, and took photographs of the wrecked sign. Once he'd finished, he explained they'd need photographic evidence when they sued.

"Sue? But I'm not hurt."

"You're in shock. Perhaps you'll suffer PTSD."

"I'll be OK once I get home. Anyway it was an accident."

"That sign wasn't secure," Mike said. "They're negligent and it's going to cost them."

"There were some really strong gusts of wind, that's …"

"Doesn't matter. These companies have huge amounts of third party cover for exactly this kind of thing." Mike sounded quite excited and didn't seem to be paying attention to his driving.

"Where are we going? This isn't the way home."

"You collapsed back there. Obviously you're suffering more than you realise, so I'm taking you to hospital for a check up."

She just wanted to go home, but it was nice he cared enough to be worried, and the evening's events had left her feeling confused. It might be wise to get a doctor to look at her.

At the hospital, Mike went to great lengths to point out how distressed Joanna was, and to bring a tiny scratch on her face to the doctor's attention. Mike knew as well as Joanna that a neighbour's cat caused it two days previously. She was too tired to wonder if Mike was still trying to gather 'evidence' to sue someone, or just determined to get his money's worth out of the hospital check up.

Later than night, Joanna couldn't help wondering when he'd start to think the money he was paying out for her life insurance would be wasted if he didn't make a claim on the policy. Maybe it had already occurred to him? She recalled the time he'd insisted on trying to repair the old washing machine. When she'd come to use it there was a flash of brilliant blue and the power went off in the house. And she'd had terrible indigestion the last time he'd cooked …

Her dreams that night involved Mike loosening the screws on the sign above the office where she worked, bumping into her as they walked along busy streets, causing her to stumble into the traffic, and a seaside holiday from which he returned as a widower.

By the morning Joanna felt much better. Of course her husband wasn't planning to kill her. He might do it accidentally by buying short-dated food, or refusing to pay for proper tradesmen and new equipment if he thought he could mend something himself, but he'd probably start missing her once he'd filled in the claim forms. Mike didn't hate her. Perhaps he even loved her, but he loved money more. He'd been so pleased with the idea of suing a multinational company he hadn't noticed Joanna really was shaking with shock and not putting it on for the doctor's benefit.

He didn't like her going out to see her friends, because the pleasure their company gave her didn't seem to him to be worth the price of a pizza. He liked her natural look because compliments were cheaper than lipstick. To him, helping a stranger was something that should be rewarded with more than kind words.

In her lunch break the next day, Joanna walked down the High Street in search of the door she'd opened for the old lady. She found it easily. The location, colour and lock were all identical. The only difference was that it didn't open onto the stairway up to a private flat, but was the doorway to the office of a legal firm. One which, Joanna saw from a sign in the window, dealt with divorces. It made no sense at all. When she'd opened that door the previous evening, she'd seen a hallway and a red patterned stair carpet. Had she imagined that and the lady who'd dropped her key?

Real or not, the woman had probably saved Joanna's life. She felt the best way to thank her was to ensure that the rest of it was happy. She pushed open the door. As she stepped into the solicitor's office, ready to start divorce proceedings against Mike, Joanna noticed the faint scent of apples.

23. Changing Faces

"Please don't come closer," Diane whispered. She shrank into the sofa. Hard ropes dug uncomfortably into her wrists and ankles. The crudely applied bandages were, in comparison, almost comfortable. Mercifully she couldn't feel the garish bruises mottling her skin.

When Diane asked her sons what they wanted to do tonight, she'd had no idea of the horrors to come. The boys had been demanding. Diane had, as usual, taken the easy option and given in. It seemed like harmless fun, but now as she surveyed the chaos in her usually neat and tidy living room, she regretted not being firmer. Regretted? She gave a hysterical laugh.

Tatters of ripped cloth hung from the curtain tracks. The normally bright room was swathed in shadowy gloom. Diane knew what she'd already endured was just the start of a very long night. It wasn't the house or her safety that concerned her; it was the change to her sons. Hallowe'en had always seemed a silly notion, but now she had to take it seriously.

She could hardly believe she'd created the monsters who now faced her. Were her darling boys still there under the pallid skin? Was it really them looking out from those red-rimmed eyes, sunken into dark shadows? Glancing away from their ravaged faces, she saw their ripped clothing, liberally stained with something deep red and sticky.

The three edged nearer, making inhuman groaning

sounds.

"Please, don't hurt me," she pleaded.

The advance halted for a moment. They laughed.

As one, the three creatures raised their arms with hands outstretched, as though insisting she give them something. Although she'd sometimes had to deny them the latest expensive toy, or the priciest designer trainers, she'd always given them love, food and shelter. What more could she do? She'd tried to bring them up well and teach right from wrong. People always blame the parents, especially if she's a single mother.

"Are you scared?" Damien, the tallest asked.

Karl, the middle boy leant forward and stared into her face. As she watched transfixed, his eyes rolled back to reveal ghostly white orbs, streaked with blood. Diane gasped in disgust. Karl laughed horribly.

What should she say? Clearly they wanted to frighten her; was that all they wanted? If she confessed to feelings of terror perhaps they'd be satisfied? It was worth a try.

"Yes, I'm frightened."

Frank, the smallest, giggled. "Scaredy scaredy."

The three edged closer.

"Give us what we want, or pay the price," Damien demanded.

What could she possibly give them? Was there anything in the house that could possibly calm them down?

The dreadful trio moved as one until close enough to touch and to smell.

Diane put her arms up in front of her. That's when she saw the fingers she'd used to touch them, had become the same pale colour as theirs and now had the same greasy texture. A trickle of the deep red liquid oozed down her arm and there was a small pool of it on the floor by her feet.

Diane screamed.

"Sorry, Mum," Frank said.

"We didn't really mean to scare you, we were just pretending," Karl said.

"Gotcha!" Diane said in triumph. "I was pretending too."

The boys gave horrid groans, then hugged her.

"You've done a fantastic job with our costumes and face painting," Damien said. "We'll help clear up the mess before we go out trick or treating. And don't worry, you won't be on your own. When we tell the other kids about your brilliant costume and the way you've decorated the house, they'll all come round to see."

Diane laughed. "I can hardly wait! Now off you go and have fun."

24. Pedalo Number Seven

Bird shaped pedalos floated in the pond all year round. Brilliantly coloured ducks, glistening white swans, palid flamingoes and a couple of grey ones I supposed were gulls. I saw them every day; the park is between home and the hospital.

When it was wet and cold, the pedalos stayed in the centre as though huddling together for warmth. On fine days some of them were brought to the edge, where children could pay over pocket money to have a go. Number seven was never among them.

Then Kate went into remission. She was stronger than she'd been for months. The look of joy on her face when I suggested going to the park broke my heart. Again. The pieces must have been almost too small to see by then, but the pain hadn't reduced.

Kate pointed towards the pond. "Please, Mummy."

I knew she'd quickly become exhausted. Perhaps Bill, the pedalo man, would need to wade in and rescue her. But, for a minute or two beforehand, she'd feel just like any other child. Happy and free.

How could I refuse?

I offered the money. Bill gave a 'hold on' gesture then paddled his little dinghy over to fetch number seven. He held it steady as I lifted Kate in. I wanted to pedal for her, but there's not room for two.

When I saw the pedalo glide away I could almost believe Kate had a hope of recovery. She looked as serene as the swan her little craft represented. The other kids pumped their legs, trying to go as fast as they could. Kate just seemed to float. She looked so happy. Looked almost healthy.

Although I didn't understand why my daughter's huge smile should make me cry, my eyes blurred with tears. The pond isn't big, but it was crowded and for a few moments I lost track of Kate.

Every now and again Bill called a variation of, "Come in number three. Your time is up."

He only called if there was another child waiting, otherwise he let them go round and round until they'd had enough and came back themselves. That day there was a queue, but still number seven wasn't called in.

Eventually Kate drifted back and I lifted her out. Her eyes were shining and her cheeks flushed pink. As I wheeled her back to the car, Kate's words tumbled over each other as she told me about the wonderful adventure she's been on.

"I sailed to an island and ran along the beach. The sand was so warm and soft. I swam with turtles and climbed trees to pick fruit."

"That sounds wonderful." Just like her imagination. I suppose being stuck in the hospital unable to do much made her that way.

Every time Kate was well enough, she begged to go to the park and ride the pedalos. Eleven more times we went over that final year. She was always given pedalo number seven. Somehow I knew Kate was safe on it. I could relax for a few minutes and look about me. Watch the leaves fall, or woodsmoke drift across from the allotments. There was always a moment I lost sight of Kate.

Always she came back with tales of her wonderful island. Then the day came when she drifted away from life. She was barely conscious but I knew she could hear me. I told her we'd go to the park and she'd ride on her swan again. I knew it couldn't happen, but meant every word.

So without her I went to the pond and held out my money. There were empty pedalos but Bill paddled to the centre and brought me number seven. It was a struggle to squeeze in, but comfortable once I'd managed. At first I floated across the pond. Then a flurry of sleet blocked my view. When it cleared the sky was brilliant blue and the air gloriously warm. In the distance I saw an island with golden sands and exotic trees just right for climbing. I pedalled furiously. As I neared the beach I saw Kate running along the golden sand, leaping high to avoid the turtles. Even over the sound of the waves breaking onto the shore, I heard her laughter.

Next thing I knew, the air was icy cold and sky grey again. Bill called, "Come in number seven." The island had gone and I drifted back to the edge of the pond.

Bill helped me out. "Your time isn't up yet," he explained. "She'll be waiting for you when it is."

The bird shaped pedalos are still in the pond in the park all year round. Multi-coloured ducks, pristine white swans, slightly gaudy pink flamingoes, and a couple of grey ones which might be geese. I see them almost every day. The park is between home and the school where I now work.

When it's wet and cold, they still cluster in the centre as though huddling together for warmth. In term time they stay there all day, every day.

At weekends or during the holidays, I go down to the park and help Bill. It's my fault the flamingoes are more cerise than subtle. They needed brightening up, but I went too far.

He didn't seem to mind.

Now it's usually me who paddles out on the dinghy and brings some of the pedalos to the edge, where children pay Bill their pocket money to have a go. On sunny days I release almost all of them. Never number seven.

One day soon, I know Bill will take a ride in it. I'll lose sight of him for a moment, then he'll return and tell me of the paradise he's found. Soon after he'll be gone for good and the pedalos will be mine until I take my final ride out to join Kate on her island. Not yet though. Our time isn't up yet.

Thank you for reading this book. I hope you enjoyed it. If you did, I'd really appreciate it if you could leave a short review on Amazon and/or Goodreads.

To learn more about my writing life, hear about new releases and get a free exclusive ebook, sign up to my newsletter – subscribepage.io/ItLSNa or you can find the link on my website patsycollins.co.uk

<u>More books by Patsy Collins</u>

Novels

Firestarter
Escape To The Country
A Year And A Day
Paint Me A Picture
Leave Nothing But Footprints
Acting Like A Killer

Little Mallow cosy mystery series

Disguised Murder and Community Spirit in Little Mallow
Dependable Friends and Deceitful Neighbours
in Little Mallow
Deadly Words and Innocent Gossip in Little Mallow

Non-fiction

From Story Idea To Reader
(co-written with Rosemary J. Kind)

A Year Of Ideas:
365 sets of writing prompts and exercises

Short story collections

Over The Garden Fence
Up The Garden Path
Through The Garden Gate
In The Garden Air
Beyond The Garden Gate

No Family Secrets
Can't Choose Your Family
Keep It In The Family
Family Feeling
Happy Families

All That Love Stuff
With Love And Kisses
Lots Of Love
Love Is The Answer

Slightly Spooky Stories I
Slightly Spooky Stories II
Slightly Spooky Stories IV
Slightly Spooky Stories V

Just A Job
Perfect Timing
A Way With Words
Dressed To Impress
Coffee & Cake
Not A Drop To Drink
Criminal Intent
Crime In Mind
Making A Move
Days To Remember
A Clean Bill Of Health
Your Good Health